ATTITUDE TOWARDS SCIENCE OF SECONDARY SCHOOL STUDENTS

Attitude Towards Science of Secondary School Students

Savita Mishra

GenNext Publication

Published by

GenNext Publication
5, Ansari Road
Daryaganj, New Delhi-110002
Phone: 011-47034999, 9811692060
E-mail: gennextpublication@hotmail.com

Distribution Network
gyanbooks.com
India, USA, Canada, UK, Australia, France

ISBN: 978-93-5663-918-8 (PB)

First Published, 2024

Printed at: Gyan Press, Delhi.

Attitude Towards Science of Secondary School Students
Author: Savita Mishra

Contents

Preface

Success is a word which enchants everybody alike–be it rich or poor, rural or urban, young or old. Success is defined and understood by different people in different way. The indisputable commonalities however remain that success requires lot of hard work and right kind of attitude. Infact, attitude precedes the hard work. Unless. you have attitude (positive), you cannot convince yourself to hard work. It is more so for young mind, when they know and understand very little about success and what it would mean to them in the long run.

I congratulate you for your decision to possess' this book, which deals with various dimensions of the attitude towards science of the students. The attitude of students towards science is affected by a variety of factors. These factors include gender, socio-economic status, their origin- rural or urban, nature of school–Government or private, etc. Interestingly, the study revealed that neither the socio-economic status nor the combined impact of socio- economic status and intelligence affected students' attitude towards science.

It is hoped that the book will help all those concerned with child's career$_{ll}$ The book is expected to help the guardians in developing right kind of attitude towards studies–especially in. science to their wards; teacher and teacher educators in analyzing the attitude of students and inculcating positive attitude towards their chosen field of study; research scholars in carrying out further in-depth studies in this field; policy makers in formulating appropriate policy towards developing positive attitude; government for announcing apprq.priate' plans; and a host of other users for attaining coveted success in their chosen field of activity.

We will feel rewarded if the parents could make use of the book by engaging themselves in inculcating positive attitude towards science of their wards in an early age. A positive attitude towards science is likely to improve students' academic perfprmance not only in science, but in other subjects, as well.

Last but not the least, the mammoth task of bringing out the book for general public would not have been possible without the co-operation and support rendered by Dr PL Mohapatra, my illustrious guide. Similarly, Shri B K Jha, my husband, who not only encouraged me to publish this piece of work but also edited and fine-tuned the material to make it precise and align it in its proper perspective. The publishers M/s Kalpaz Publications, Delhi also deserve appreciation for readily acceding to our request.

(Dr. Savita Mishra)

Introduction

Education in the present day context is perhaps the single most important means for individuals to improve personal endowments, build capacity levels, overcome constraints, and in the process, enlarge their available set of opportunities and choices for a sustained improvement and well-being. Education is important not merely as means to other ends, but it is an attitude that is valued in itself by most people.

The progress, welfare and prosperity of a nation depend on rapid, planned and sustained growth in the quality and extent of education and research in science and technology. Science based education in coherence with Indian culture and values can provide the foundations and the instrument for the nation's progress, security and welfare. Jawaharlal Nehru, the first Prime Minister of India was of the opinion (1960) that science alone can solve the problems of hunger and poverty, insanitation and illiteracy, superstition and deadening customs and tradition, vast resources running waste of a rich country inhabited by the starving people. Indira Gandhi, considered(1982) that science is of deeper significance as it has not only altered man's material environment but influenced the basic values of life and added new vitality and dynamism to civilisation.

Science and technology have opened the doors to the world of new thought and meaningful action. Science has brought about revolutionary changes in every walk of our life. Its impact is visible everywhere and in every aspect of our existence, i.e., vocational, social, economic, political and cultural. We have become dependent upon science not only for industrial productions, communication, defence, medicine, transport but also domestic amenities and agriculture.

Most of the countries which popularised science among the adolescents have become modern and advance and thus influenced the entire universe as compared to those, which do not or lately introduced science in their system of education. Realising the importance, various education commissions and committees formed by our National Government have recommended for modernising the system of teaching science at every level. There has been significant improvement in science teaching in India after 1970. Throughout the country, whole curriculum in science underwent change with the broader objectives of providing adequate knowledge to the students about the physical and biological world around them in order to enable them to take intelligent decisions.

1.1 *Importance of Science Education*

The endeavour of science has been successful in achieving its objectives except the values and ethics of science, which requires to be nurtured in the younger generation and needs proper attention and honest attempt by the teachers, teacher educators and educational policy makers. The most important of these values and ethics is the attitude towards science, which is one of the most important objectives of science teaching and learning at school level. Science education is extremely important for the growth and development of the world but it is equally important that it should be taught applying right transactional strategies so that it can nurture right kind of values and much desired attitude towards science, which has the potential to eliminate superstition and other evils of the society and may solve a host of problems.

If we have attitude towards science and if we consider this in our day to day life situations, we can refine our family life, social life, political life, economic spheres etc., and thus can bring peace and harmony in our society. The present world has perceived the importance of science for all the global citizens. This is the reason that slogans , "Science for all" and "Scientific literacy" are being widely talked about at global arena.

Most of the changes of our country have been affected by science and technology. In reality, science, more than any other subject in the traditional school curriculum, has been closely associated with economic and social development of our society. Science education offers a knowledge-based way of knowing which can be applied for effective solution of human environmental problems and to industrial development.Science education enlightens the young generation in the following areas of knowledge:

- Knowledge of science for healthy living –personal as well as social.
- Knowledge of science for agriculture.
- Knowledge of science for ecological balance.
- Knowledge of science for nutrition.
- Knowledge of science for clean environment and it's protection.
- Knowledge of science for job requirement.

Science, therefore, occupies a very important place in curriculum both at school and university stages of education in India. Science education is supposed to perform a two-fold task. First of all, in individual perspective, the cultivation of a scientific temper, spirit of enquiry, disposition to reason logically, habit of judging beliefs and formation of opinions based on available evidence, readiness to reject unfounded theories and principles have been emphasised in science education. Similarly, in the social perspective, science education aims at equipping individuals to participate in the creation of a society which is free from poverty, hunger, diseases and evils such as violence, exploitation, oppression, etc.

Science education in schools prepares pupils to deal with the innumerable problems of life with a scientific attitude. Including science, as one of the subjects in the school curriculum is not enough, maximising the achievement of pupils in science is the main concern of science education.

The primary task in science education must include the transaction of activities which need to be simple, clear and unequivocal, so as to eliminate doubt, uncertainty and difficulty. Secondly, it conducts test which aims at discovering what the students actually know and how far they are capable of applying the knowledge in their lives and activities. There are numerous advantages of science education e.g., (i) thinking and memory develops, (ii) principles are formulated, (iii) self-confidence and self-reliance develop, (iv) love for truth enhances, (v) confidence regarding unity in diversity increases, (vi) devotion towards nature increases, (vii) avenues open for newer and newer vocations. Besides these advantages, science has become the basis of our cultural heritage and social progress. Not only like other disciplines, education being an independent discipline of study, is placed in the faculty of science. This is the reason why education is not only an art but science also. Most of the principles of modern education are scientific and almost all the strategies, tactics and techniques of teaching are going to be scientific in nature today. Science is based on the principle that there is a real, self-consistent world, that scientific experiences are reproducible, that they are accessible to falsification, and they should not contradict established laws of science. Science should not be distorted to fit the prevailing views of the time. The Big Bang Theory of the origin of the universe was not devised to fit the scriptures but to explain the evidence. There is some unknown, but as science advances the unknown becomes part of the known, but more unknown comes.

Man's journey of life in this world is wonderful. Science is a journey towards the truth and we know that truth will make everybody fresh and free. The study of nature, through multiple discipline of science, makes it all the more exciting and fascinating. Every student of science can experience this excitement if he or she asks the right questions and seeks a logical answer to each of the questions. Once we develop the habit of understanding things, we would not blindly accept facts and information and would thus develop attitude towards science. Scientific knowledge and scientific temper, both form a right combination and are the key for development. Teaching of science at school stage helps in development of scientific literacy. It also helps in the formations of scientific attitude, which is essential to dispel social evils and helps in development of open mindedness and decision taking ability. Training in scientific method thus improves the quality of thinking.

The failure in examinations and low achievement in science is very much baffling. Many studies revealed that factors such as intelligence, attitude, socio-economic status, study habits and other correlates of the school are the non-intellectual factors which affect achievement. There is significant difference in the achievement of pupils in science studying in rural and urban schools. The Education Commission of 1964-66 remarks, "If science is poorly taught and badly learnt, it is like little more than burdening the mind with dead information and it could degenerate into a new superstition. What we need is improvement in the standard and quality of science education at all levels in the country". Better science education naturally demands better facilities for providing it. The essential provisions needed for effective science education are:

- An up-to-date, dynamic science syllabus.
- A properly qualified willing teacher who loves the subject and the learners.
- Essential science material and equipment.
- A well-equipped rich laboratory.
- A programme of curricular and co-curricular activities to supplement the class room teaching.

The development and prosperity of any country depends on the ability of that country to utilise the up-to-date knowledge of technology. The developing countries like India are depending on advanced countries for technical assistance. But no country having self-respect can afford to rely on foreign assistance for a long time. Hence, India has to build up a sound system of science education at all levels.

In general terms science education can be said to include the aims to impart information and provide a context for theory, train the powers of observation, memory, expressions, skill of reasoning and logical investigations. This is because the notion of questioning, investigating the questions and communicating the results are often defined as important aspects of the scientific enterprise and of the nature of science itself. However, there is more to learning science than gaining knowledge and developing skills. The area of the affective, the personal acceptance and enjoyment of and commitment to the scientific activities is of central importance in doing science. Doing science is a holistic activity involving the will and the imagination as well as the hand and the mind.

By virtue of the scientific method or the systematic process, science can only be an instrument in solving present and future human problems. It is the human, who actually solves his own problems with the help of science. So it is necessary for them to know what the scientist do so as to make one familiar with the scientific facts and principles. In view of this, a sound system of science education, from the lowest level of schooling becomes imperative. It has, therefore, been included in the elementary as well as secondary stages of education, but its quality has to be improved at all costs.

Every individual in a democracy like India must be benefited by the knowledge of science for various considerations. Some such points are enumerated below:

- Science education can assist the individual in making adjustment to new conditions arising from the fast moving scientific advancement and discovery.
- Science education can develop the rational thought process in the citizens which would lead to a better social order.

- The laws of science form the basis of universal understanding irrespective of language, colour and religion.
- Science education can offer the individual an introduction to the broad area of physical and biological phenomena and many other aesthetic features as well as sense of appreciation.

On account of the multifarious values of science and its contribution to development of scientific attitude towards science and scientific method, science commands a special position in the world of human knowledge and learning. It is, therefore, very much appropriate to provide and improve science education in all spheres of the country. For improving the quality of life through economic and material development, we depend on the knowledge of science. Indian Education Commission (1964-66) in the context of importance of science in school curriculum writes, "There is, of course, one thing about which we feel no doubt or hesitation: education science based and in coherence with Indian culture and values, can alone provide the foundations as also the instrument for the nation's progress, security and welfare". Development of science has paved the way for a more effective and practical mastery of the environment. The technological innovation in agriculture, industry and medicine had brought transformation in traditional pattern of social living. In the words of Indira Gandhi (1982), "Science has not only radically altered man's material environment, but it is of still deeper significance, and influenced even the basic values of life and has given to civilisation a new vitality and dynamism" to civilisation.

1.2 Inclusion of Science in School Curriculum

A few decades back, science was not relatively popular among common people. It was limited to certain class of people. Now science has established its claim to be placed in school curriculum. It has now been recognised as compulsory subject from the beginning of school education. There is now rapid change and advancement in science and technology and the growing complexity of industrial and economic organisation, there is increasing demand for larger number of highly skilled and trained personnel drawn from different disciplines. They function generally in composite team, rather than as individuals. Science has thus become a part and parcel of our life and therefore more stress is to be given on science education to meet the growing demands of the society.

Science has played key role in transforming the world from prehistoric age to the present age of globalisation. The boon and the curse of science, the world has experienced is well known to the present generation. The advancement of world in the field of agriculture, industry, health facility, education and other service sectors are all because of the development of science and technology. Today's booming global economy and the development of all nations in all walks of life is directly related to the development of science and technology.

This is the information age resulted due to the explosion of knowledge and information and communication technology. This is the age of the survival of the fittest and the fastest. Science and technology are expanding at a fast rate and has become inseparable part of human activities. Now the life cannot be imagined without science and its products.

Science is very useful subject in the school and the range of usefulness extended from simple problem in daily life to complex problems in various branches of higher scientific studies. We are living in an age of science and technology. If our country is to instep with rapidly changing world then;

- First of all, our school must be able to prepare students who can master efficiently the latest development in all fields of science and technologies are being discovered every year.
- Secondly, our school curriculum should adhere to the scientific values to enhance the pragmatic attitude among the pupil.
- Thirdly, secondary school is an appropriate stage for the initiation of the future scientist, it is essential that the teaching of science must have a prominent place in the secondary school of our country.

According to Education Commission Report (1966), at the secondary level, science as a discipline of the mind and a preparation for higher education deserves special emphasis. In the lower secondary classes, Physics, Chemistry, Biology and Earth Science should be taught as compulsory subject for the entire pupil. Building on the introductory courses at the earlier stages, they should cover wider areas and go deeper into content than before. The changing character of the science should be the major factor in curriculum development.

National Policy on Education (1986) has taken science as one of the subject in the core curriculum for ten years schooling. Thus, children need to possess considerable knowledge of science to understand its influence on human affair. Some of the reasons to include science as a school subject are as follows:

- In this "science and technology oriented" society, every citizen should be able to understand the role of science in agriculture, food, health, energy, industry, environment and ecological concerns. It is evident that the proper development in science can only occur if citizens are informed and are able to contribute to the making of decision involving science-based issue.

- The understanding of science and technology needs, decision making ability about personal hygiene, nutrition, safety, disposal of waste product, control of pollution and the industrial hazards.
- Understanding of importance of science for society, in relation to economic, industrial and social aspects.
- Science satisfies the curiosity of learner through its ever increasing sphere of knowledge and innovations.
- Science has a direct bearing on the social aspect which is related to living including ethical, social and moral aspect of life.
- Science has its value such as objectivity and rationality. Its application in agriculture, industries and allied fields has increased the productivity of the nation.
- The revised National Policy on Education (1992) has observed that there is erosion of essential values and the increasing dynamism in society has brought to focus the need for readjustments in curriculum, in order to make education a forceful tool for the cultivation of social and moral values.
- Education as an organised social system has an important function in the development of moral, spiritual and aesthetic values. In science classroom too, a science teacher cannot avoid dealing with values. The values are to be inculcated among the student through science education effectively so as to make them a true citizen of the nation.

1.3 Concept of Attitude towards Science

The term attitude begins as a relatively simple one-dimensional concept consisting of the affective component of psychological object and has grown into a complex multi-dimensional concept consisting of the three domains of experience, cognitive, affective and conative.

Attitudes are ethics. How one is disposed towards a particular thing, place or a person reflects one's attitudes. An attitude is hence a condition of mind that brings in imagination and emotional states which are the outcome of previous experience. Attitudes condition behaviour and therefore are of paramount importance in education. Thurston and Chave (1929) defined attitude as sum total of a man's behaviour and feelings, prejudice and biased, preconceived notion, ideas, threats and convictions about any specific activities, it defers from opinion which means a verbal statement hypothesised to be symptomatic of attitude. In other words attitude is what you feel and opinion is what you express. These may be general or specific.

In the fast moving world and conflicting demand of the society, individual is faced with more and more problem that had made difficult to adjust. Therefore, there is a need for developing right sort of attitude to avoid any mental conflicts. One of the most important attitude that must be inculcated in students to make them useful and socially efficient citizens is the scientific attitude that can profitably developed through various subjects in general and in science subjects in particular. Because developing attitude towards science is potential means of eliminating intolerance, superstitions, obscurantism which are considered socially undesirable.

Development of attitude towards science is one of the most important objectives of science teaching at school level all over the world. Scientific thinking and attitude towards science are not reserved solely for scientist. Anyone can "think like a scientist" who learns the scientific method and, most importantly, applies its precepts, whether he or she is investigating nature or not. When one uses the methods and principles of scientific thinking in everyday life, such as when studying history or literature, investigating societies or governments, seeking solutions to problems of economic or philosophy or just trying to answer personal questions about oneself or the meaning of existence one is said to be practicing critical thinking. Critical thinking is necessarily involves objective thinking so as to arrive at most reliable answers to questions and solutions to problems. In other words, critical thinking may help to have reliable knowledge about all aspects of one's life and society by allowing one to explore and consider all dimensions of a given issue or a problem. Thus, critical thinking is not restricted to only the formal study of nature. Professional in humanities, social sciences, jurisprudence, business, and journalism also practice critical thinking like any scientist.

The investigation of students' attitudes towards studying science has been a substantive feature of the work of the science education research community for the past 30–40 years. Consequently, the promotion of favourable attitudes towards science, scientists and learning science, which has always been a component of science education, is increasingly a matter of concern. However, the concept of an attitude towards science is somewhat nebulous, often poorly articulated and not well understood.

Concerns about attitudes to science are not new. Nearly 30 years ago, Ormerod and Duckworth (1975) began their review on the topic of pupils' attitudes to science in the UK with the following comment: In 1965 a thorough inquiry began into the flow of students of science and technology in higher education. The final report (Dainton, 1968) laid particular emphasis on the phenomenon which had become known as the 'swing from science'. Several explanations were suggested for the swing, among them a lessening interest in science and disaffection with science and technology amongst students.

In the intervening period, particularly the past decade, evidence would suggest that the problem has become even more acute and the topic has been the subject of considerable exploration, both at an empirical and theoretical level, although predominantly in the US. As a consequence, our understanding of the nature of the problem has possibly improved, although possibly not our understanding of its remediation (Osborne, 2003).

Even a cursory examination of the domain reveals that one of the most prominent aspects of the literature is that 30 years of research into this topic has been bedevilled by a lack of clarity about the concept under investigation. An early notable contribution towards its elaboration was made by Klopfer (1971), who categorised a set of affective behaviours in science education as:

- The manifestation of favourable attitudes towards science and scientists;
- The acceptance of scientific enquiry as a way of thought;
- The adoption of 'scientific attitudes';
- The enjoyment of science learning experiences;
- The development of interests in science and science-related activities; and

- The development of an interest in pursuing a career in science or science related work.

Gardner (1975) classified the basic distinction between 'attitudes towards science' and 'scientific attitudes'. Attitudes towards science refers to the feelings, beliefs and values held about an object that may be the enterprise of science, school science, the impact of science on society or scientists. Attitudes towards science do not consist of a single unitary construct, but a large number of sub-constructs all of which contribute in varying proportions towards an individual's attitudes towards science. Studies (Breakwell and Beardsell 1992; Brown 1976; Crawley and Black 1992; Gardner 1975; Haladyna, Olsen, and Shaughnessy 1982; Keys 1987; Koballa Jr. 1995; Oliver and Simpson 1988; Ormerod and Duckworth 1975; Piburn 1993; Talton and Simpson 1985, 1986, 1987; Woolnough 1994) have incorporated a range of components in their measures of attitudes to science including:

- the perception of the science teacher;
- anxiety toward science;
- the value of science;
- self-esteem at science;
- motivation towards science;
- enjoyment of science;
- attitudes of peers and friends towards science;
- attitudes of parents towards science;
- the nature of the classroom environment;
- achievement in science; and
- fear of failure on course.

Attitude towards science refers to subject's preferences and feelings. Whereas scientific attitudes are a complex mixture of the longing to know and understand, a questioning approach to all statements, a search for data and their meaning, a demand for verification, a respect for logic, a consideration of premises and a consideration of consequences, (Gauld and Hukins,1980), (Education Policies Commission, 1962). Scientific attitudes are the features that might be said to characterise scientific thinking and are cognitive in nature.

However, of themselves, they will not necessarily be related to the behaviours a pupil actually exhibits. For, as several commentators have pointed out (Brown, 1976; Potter and Wetherall, 1987), behaviour may be influenced by the fact that attitudes other than the ones under consideration may be more strongly held; motivation to behave in another way may be stronger than the motivation associated with the expressed attitude; or, alternatively, the anticipated consequences of a specific behaviour may modify that behaviour so that it is inconsistent with the attitude held (e.g., a pupil may express interest in science but avoid publicly demonstrating it among his/her peers who regard such an expression of intellectual interest as not being the 'done thing').

Consequently, it is behaviour rather than attitude that has become a focus of interest and that has led researchers to explore models developed from studies in social psychology; in particular, Ajzen and Fishbein's (1980) theory of reasoned action, which is concerned fundamentally with predicting behaviour. This theory focuses on the distinction between attitudes towards some 'object' and attitudes towards some specific action to be performed towards that 'object' (e.g., between attitudes towards science and attitudes towards doing school science). Ajzen and Fishbein argue that it is the latter kind of attitude that best predicts behaviour. Thus, their theory represents a relationship between attitude, intention and behaviour. Behaviour is seen as being determined by intention, and intention, in turn, is a joint product of attitude towards the behaviour and the subjective norm (i.e. beliefs about how other people would regard one's performance of the behaviour). The theory of reasoned action has been successfully applied to some attitude and behaviour studies in science education (for example, Crawley and Black, 1992; Crawley and Coe, 1990; Norwich and Duncan, 1990). For instance, Crawley and Coe (1990), Koballa Jr. (1988) and Oliver and Simpson (1988) have all found that social support from peers and attitude towards enrolling for a course are strong determinants of student choice to pursue science courses voluntarily, which suggests that the theory has at least some partial validity. The main value of such a theory is its help in determining salient beliefs that can then be reinforced or downplayed to affect relevant behavioural decisions by students such as 'girls don't do science'. Furthermore, this theory points towards the need to draw a demarcation between school science and science in society. It is the perception of school science, and the feelings towards the 'behaviour' of undertaking a further course of study in that context, which are most significant in determining children's decisions about whether to proceed with further study of science post-16.

However, ultimately, some doubt is cast on what is being measured by the many instruments that have been devised to assess attitude. Potter and Wetherall (1987), arguing from qualitative data on attitudes toward race, show convincingly that attitude instruments measure only one aspect of individual's views. Rather, any good understanding of attitude towards an object is only revealed by a study of the attitude in the context of its use. In essence, what Potter and Wetherall's work points to that many attitude instruments only measure what is the tip of the iceberg – the most obvious and evidently displayed attitudes towards an object. Fundamentally, attitude cannot be separated from its context and the underlying body of influences that determine its real significance. In the case of school science, this points to the need to move away from general quantitative measures of attitude constructs and instead, to explore the specific issue of students' attitudes to *school science*, and their attitude to studying further courses in *science in school* with a view to gaining information of their effect on student subject choice.

The scientific method has proven to be the most reliable and successful method of thinking in human history, and it is quite possible to use scientific thinking in all human endeavours. Critical thinking is perhaps the most important skill a student can learn in school and college. If a person masters this skill, he learns how to think successfully and reach to a reliable conclusion, and such ability will prove valuable in any human endeavour.

A person with attitude towards science reflects the behaviour, as shown in figure (i), in his or her personality while dealing with diverse kinds of situation. If we look at Fig.1.1 and think deeply, we can find that we can solve all problems be it political, economic, social or otherwise provided that all the parties to the concerned problem have attitude towards science and they use it while solving the problems (School Science,Vol. 46, No. 4, 33).

In modern time, the chief aim of education is to enable a citizen to develop scientific attitude towards science of mind to think objectively and base his

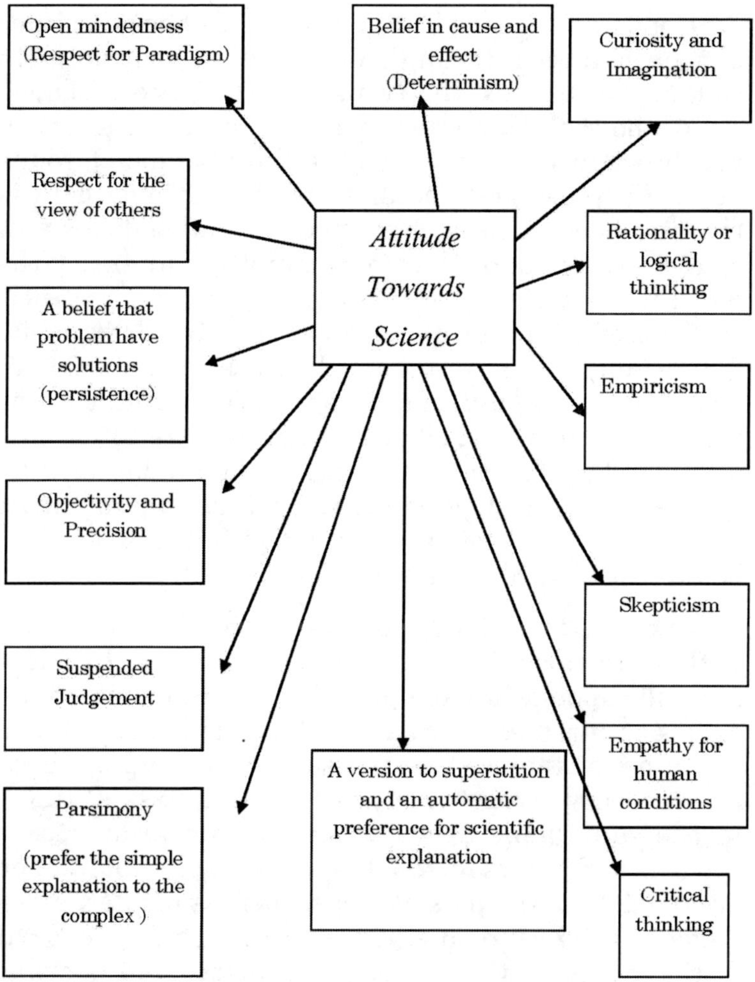

Fig. 1.1: Components of Attitude towards Science (School Science, Vol. 46, No. 4, 33).

conclusion on tested data. By developing attitude towards science in a person, certain mind sets created in a particular direction. Such mind sets are may be developed either by direct teaching in school or by out of school experiences gained by the people. Attitude are developed and learned, they are not in born. Attitude can be changed through experiences especially in children. These are the result of experiences. Though out of the school experiences contribute to large extent yet direct teaching does modify the attitude of young pupil. Attitudes are mental state or individual outlook towards, people, object, events etc. The attitude towards science (ATS) may be operationally taken as the generalised attitude towards the universe of science, content of which is being measured in terms of its favourableness or unfavourableness. Allport (1935) opines that, "the attitude towards science refers to the feelings, opinions, beliefs in and about appreciation that an individual forms as a result of interacting directly or indirectly with various aspect of the scientific enterprises and which exerts a direct influence on their behaviour towards science."

Attitude towards science refers to an individual's outlook towards life. It means willingness to adopt scientific approaches and procedure for resolving issues, assessing ideas or information. Attitude is defined as a condition, a stabilised mental set which expresses itself in a tendency to react to any member of a class of stimuli in the same general way. Attitude towards science predisposes a person to engage in responsible action after weighing the possible consequences of alternative, options, using rational arguments based on evidence. It distinguishes between scientific evidence and personal option and between reliable and unreliable information remains open to new evidence and the tentativeness of scientific knowledge and recognises that science and technology are human endeavours. Some other manifestations of the attitude towards science are questioning, suspension of judgement, appraisal of different sides of an issue, verification of knowledge, curiosity and appreciation of the natural and human made world, open mindedness, intellectual, honesty, co-operation and tolerance of the point of view of other people. The attitude towards science presents a systematic account of the cognitive and social feature of science. Attitude embraces three distinct components: the affective, the behavioural and the cognitive. According to Koballa (1990), attitudes are learned either actively or vicariously and therefore, can be taught. Hence essentially, attitude towards science involve feelings, opinions, beliefs and appreciation, which individuals have formed as a result of interacting directly and indirectly with various aspect of the scientific enterprise (Hasan Bilch, 1975; Munby, 1983). It also covers emotional reactions, someone exhibit towards science. The term "scientific attitudes," on the other hand is perceived as desirable attribute of scientists in professional work and could be categorised as interest, adjustment, appreciation as well as values. These attributes include suspended judgement, curiosity open mindedness, intellectual, honesty, critical mindedness, skepticism, rationality, objectivity and questioning attitudes (Kozlow and Nay, 1974).

Spread of attitude towards science in society is much more than the spread of science and technology. Attitude towards science is neither a collection of knowledge or facts, although it promotes such knowledge; nor is it rationalism although it promotes rational thinking. It is something more. It is an attitude of mind which calls for a particular outlook and pattern of behaviour. It is of universal applicability and has to permeate through our society as the dominant value system, powerfully influencing the way we think and approach our problems—political, social, economic, cultural and educational. The spirit of inquiry and the acceptance of the right to question and be questioned are fundamental to attitude towards science. It calls upon one to ask the 'how' the 'what' and the 'why' of an object, event or phenomenon. It further calls upon one to exercise the right to question, provided of course, the questioning of an existing theory, hypotheses, or statement or social situation is done in accordance with the scientific method and is not merely a base assertion of one's belief. Attitude towards science is, therefore, incompatible with the acceptance of authorities of all kinds or of 'high priests' who may not be questioned. It leads to the realisation that events occur as a result of interplay of understandable and desirable natural and social forces and not because someone, however great, so ordained them. These forces are often complex and intertwined and have to be analytically disentangled.

Attitude towards science is compatible with observation and insight, reasoning and intuition, systematic work and creative impulse. It gives rise to an attitude of mind which while being conscious of vast areas of ignorance, is nevertheless, optimistic about human ability to gradually unravel the mysteries that surround us. In this process, attitude towards science becomes a part of the culture, a philosophy, and a way of life which leads to pursuit of truth without prejudgment. Attitude towards science implies the recognition that knowledge often progresses by disproving earlier ideas, beliefs, theories and laws. It considers knowledge as open ended and ever evolving. It lays emphasis on verifiability and repeatability, wherever possible and on the fact that scientific theories, laws and facts allow one to make predictions which can be tested. It recognises that answers to too many questions that may be asked at any given time may not be available at that time. It then demands the courage and humility to say, "I do not know". Inherent in attitude towards science is a system of value judgments. The inculcation of attitude towards science in our society would result in our people becoming rational and objective, thereby generating a climate favouring an egalitarian, democratic, secular and universalistic outlook. Consequently, scientific attitude cannot flourish in a grossly in egalitarian society where 50 per cent of the population lives below the poverty line and almost 70 per cent of our people, especially females are illiterate. Social justice, widespread education and unrestricted communication are therefore pre-requisites for spread of attitude towards science and for optimising the results of science and technology.

1.4 *Components of Attitude Towards Science*

One of the major aims of teaching sciences is the development of attitude towards science in the pupil. Following are some of the various aspects included in the attitude towards science:

- Making pupils open minded;
- Helping pupils make critical observations;
- Developing intellectual honesty among pupils;
- Developing curiosity among pupils;
- Developing unbiased and impartial thinking;
- Developing reflective thinking.

NSSE (National Society of the Study of Education) has defined attitude towards science as "open mindedness, a desire for accurate knowledge, confidence in procedures for seeking knowledge and the expectation that the solution of the problem will come through the use of verified knowledge". The views regarding attitude towards science expressed at a workshop conducted by the National Council of Educational Research and Training (NCERT) at Chandigarh in 1971 can be summarised as follows. A pupil who has developed attitude towards science:

- Is clear and precise in his activities and makes clear and precise statements;
- Always bases his judgement on verified facts and not on opinions;
- Prefers to suspend his judgement if sufficient data is not available;
- Is objective in his approach and behaviour;
- Is free from superstitions;
- Is honest and truthful in recording and collecting scientific data;
- After finishing his work takes care to arrange the apparatus, equipment etc., at their proper places;
- Shows a favourable reaction towards efforts of using science for human welfare.

Thus, from the above discussion, it can be said that the following are the components of attitude towards science:

- Elimination of belief in superstitions;
- Curiosity to know;
- Open mindedness;
- Facts with proofs;
- Critical evaluation;
- Accuracy in observation;
- Change of opinion after getting evidence;
- Attitude to discover;
- Respect for other views;
- Biased/Prejudiced notions.

The list is only suggestive and not exhaustive. The sole responsibility of developing attitude towards science lies on the teacher who can manipulate all the situations to inspire pupils. The characteristic features of attitude towards science at the same time present himself as an example for his intellectual honesty, respect for other's point of view, unbiased and impartial behaviour in his dealings. This will create a favourable and permanent impression on students to adopt the same attitude which the teacher is having. The teacher can develop attitude towards science amongst the students in the context of curriculum, physical facilities and opportunities for practical work.

1.5 Rationale of the Study

Advancement in science and technology has created a greater demand for more people to study science and this is particularly pertinent in developing countries like India. To ensure the influx of new scientists, it is important to view how science is taught in school and this approach affects students' willingness to take an active role in science learning. Research has consistently shown attitudes as an important component of science education. Science teaching is essential for any nation to grow and compete with the global trend. The sole responsibility of developing attitude towards science among the students lies on the teacher who can manipulate all the situations to instil in pupils the characteristic features of attitude towards science and at the same time present himself as an example to the students for his intellectual honesty, respect for other points of views, unbiased and impartial behaviour. Attitude towards science was reflected through the behaviour and action of the persons who were open minded experiment oriented, systematic in approach, intellectually honest, unbiased and truthful and possesses scientific temper. Development of right kind of attitude should therefore be given due importance in the transaction of teaching – learning processes in schools. Because in this fast moving world and conflicting demands of the society, every individual is faced with more and more problems that have made him more difficult to adjust and adapt to the changing and challenging environment in the struggle for better social adjustment. There is a felt need for developing right sort of attitudes to avoid any mental conflicts. These attitudes can be developed among the students through the study of various subject and learning activities in the school curriculum. But the questions arise, whether the students are getting such type of privileges in the schools to develop such attitude. Are our schools well equipped to impart training in scientific attitude to the students? Are the institutional climates of the school like science laboratories, experiments in science laboratories, improvisation of apparatus, problem-solving and independent extra reading etc., included in school curriculum for inculcating attitude towards science in the mind of the students? Are the schools trying to remove superstitions and false belief from the mind of the students by putting questions to show evidences or proof for that belief? Is attitude dependent upon the personal variables of gender, locale, father's or mother's educational and economic status? Is there any ethnic difference in the development of attitude towards science in the student? Thus, it becomes obligatory to investigate whether the attitude of students towards science is dependent upon personal and institutional variables? If so to what extent they are reflected in the mind of the students of Cuttack and Bhubaneswar city? Hence the answers to the above research questions form the rationale of the present investigation.

In the light of the above facts, the investigator is inspired to conduct a study on the problem to know whether the students have developed favourable attitude towards science as a discipline. Therefore, the problem is stated as "Attitude of Secondary School Students towards Science in relation to some Personal and Institutional Variables".

1.6 Objectives of the Study

The following objectives are formulated for the conduct of the study:

- To study the attitude towards science of secondary school students in relation to independent impact of variables (gender and socio-economic status);
- To study the difference in attitude towards science of secondary school students due to the personal variables of intelligence;
- To study the difference in attitude towards science of secondary school students due to some institutional variables like type of school, type of management, school environment and school success;
- To study the difference in attitude towards science of secondary school students in relation to combined impact of personal variables (gender and intelligence), (gender and socio-economic status) and (socio-economic status and intelligence);
- To find out the difference in attitude towards science in the secondary school students due to the interaction effect of gender, socio-economic status and intelligence.

1.7 Hypotheses of the Study

All the hypotheses are formulated in null form for testing as elucidated below:

Ho1: There is no significant difference in attitude towards science of the students in relation to gender variable.

Ho2: There is no significant difference in attitude towards science of secondary school students due to differential levels of socio-economic status.

Ho3: There exists no significant difference in attitude towards science of secondary school students in relation to differential levels of intelligence.

Ho4: There exists no significant difference in attitude towards science of secondary school students in relation to the institutional variables.

Ho5: There is no significant difference in attitude towards science of secondary school students in respect to combined impact of gender and socio-economic status.

Ho6: There is no significant difference in attitude towards science of secondary school students in respect to combined impact of gender and intelligence.

Ho7: There is no significant difference in attitude towards science of secondary school students in respect to combined impact of socio-economic status and intelligence.

Ho8: There is no significant difference in attitude towards science of secondary school students in respect to combined impact of the three variables of gender, socio-economic status and intelligence.

1.8 Delimitations of the Study

Only 10 per cent of the schools of Cuttack and Bhubaneswar city were selected at random out of 180 schools. A total sample of 400 responded for the study. The sample was taken from the same urbanised atmosphere of the twin cities in order to control the influence of any geographic variable.

1.9 Operational Definitions of the Terms

Attitude towards Science: 'Attitude towards Science' here refers to feelings, opinions, beliefs and appreciation which individuals have formed as a result of interacting directly or indirectly with the various aspects of the scientific enterprise.

Personal Variables: 'Personal variables' here refers to gender, socio-economic status (SES) and intelligence.

- **Gender:** 'Gender' refers to the boys and girls.
- **Socio-economic Status:** 'Socio-economic Status' includes the information on education, occupation and income which determine the socio-economic status of the parents of the school children as measured by Nayak's Socio-economic Status Scale (2005) and levels of Socio-economic Status have been considered under two levels - high and low.
- **Intelligence:** 'Intelligence' here refers to the General Mental Ability as measured by Group Test of General Mental Ability by Jalota (1971) and the levels of Intelligence here also categorised under high and low, as in case of Socio-economic Status.

The categorisation of the levels of socio-economic status and intelligence are made on the basis of mean (M) and Standard Deviation (SD) where higher than M + 1 SD relates to High level and less than M–1 SD is considered as the low level.

Institutional Variables: 'Institutional variables' here refer to the type of management of institutions like government and non-government, boys and girls schools and the school environmental facilities available to the students for studying science and school success based on percentage of result in the final board examination. The facilities can be categorised under two types i.e., schools having adequate and inadequate facilities. Therefore, the institutional variables may be studied under the following:

- **Type of Management:** Government and Non-Government managed schools;
- **Type of Schools:** Boys, Girls and Co-educational schools;
- **School Environment for Studying Science:** Schools having adequate facilities, schools having inadequate facilities.
- **School Success:** It is here regarded by two levels like high achieving schools and low achieving schools making a cut off line of demarcation in percentage of results done in schools more than 75 per cent as high and less than 40 per cent as low in total.

2

Studies in Attitude Towards Science

Introduction

In this chapter, a detailed review of earlier researches has been presented in accordance with the prescriptions made in APA manual 1994. The reviews have been presented year-wise and variable-wise:

2.1 Attitude Towards Science and Gender

Kar (1990), examined the problem of relationship between attitude towards and achievement in general science of class IX. It was found that distributions of the attitude score were found to be more favourably disposed towards science in boys than girls. There was positive relationship between attitude and achievement.

Rao (1990), observed that the attitude towards science in secondary school was not influenced by sex. Medium of instruction also intervened in attitude towards science.

Harty and Samuel (1990), conducted a study on exploring relationships among four science teaching learning affective attributes of sixth grade students.

These attributes are science interest, science curiosity, and self-concept of science ability. They found that gender had influenced attitude towards science.

Collis and Williams (1990), studied on cross cultural comparison of gender differences in adolescents' attitudes towards computer science and selected school subjects and found that both Canadian and Chinese students manifested gender differences in their attitudes towards computer science and mathematics. In both grades eight and twelve, boys had significantly more positive attitudes towards these subjects than did girls. However, no differences were found with regard to science among Canadian and Chinese students.

Mandila (1990) conducted a study on attitude of secondary school students towards science curriculum and its relationship with achievement motivation. Sex and locale had favourable attitude towards science curriculum. There were significant differences in scientific temper.

Darchingpuii (1990), conducted a study on science achievement, attitude towards science and problem-solving ability among secondary schools students of Aizawal. The study examined the relationships among variables such as achievement in science, attitude towards science and problem-solving ability under certain conditions like location, socio-economic status, parental education and occupation. Findings were:

- Significant relationship existed between scores on science attitude and achievement.
- Significant sex difference in science, problem-solving ability was observed.
- High SES, family facility and type of school favoured achievement in students.

Mason and Kahle (1990), conducted a study on student attitude towards science and science-related careers: A programme designed to promote a stimulating gender free learning environment and found that although these were significant changes in attitude as a function of group (i.e., control or treatment), they did not observe a difference as a function of gender.

Temple and Lips (1990), conducted a study on gender differences and similarities in attitude towards computers and found key differences regarding student attitude towards science, computers and self-confidence between school learners and mature students.

Alexander (1990), conducted a study to find differences in attitude and aptitude in science in relation to socio-economic status and scientific aptitude.

Major findings were:

- Achievement in science was due to critical thinking, scientific achievement and socio-economic status.
- No significant interaction effect between the independent variables.
- Sex differences existed.

Tamir (1990), studies on science learning of Israeli high school students and found that boys in grades nine and twelve have more positive attitudes towards science subjects than girls and they scored higher. A significant difference was found between boys and girls in physics in grades nine and twelve, whereas in Biology and Chemistry there was no such difference.

Tobias (1990), found that students did not choose science because they had a fear of cheating themselves of a 'well-rounded liberal education'. Such findings are further reinforced by the work of Munro and Elsom

(2000), which found that the compulsory nature of school science made less demand on science teachers to market their subject and, when they did, they predominantly emphasised its instrumental value rather than any cultural significance. Their findings would suggest that science teachers and many of their students, still share Matthew Arnold's nineteenth-century view that scientific training is a form of education that would produce only a 'useful specialist' and not a truly educated man (*sic*). In short, that a knowledge of science has no intrinsic cultural value as knowledge, which is an essential component for the educated woman or man.

Otto (1991), presented a very thorough discussion as to possible influenced upon females in science. He pointed out that "explanations for women not entering the science fields have focused on (i) disparity in cognitive abilities, (ii) personality characteristics, (iii) attitudes towards science, (iv) differences between in-schools and out-of-school experiences, and (v) gender differences in mathematics preparation". He pointed out that attitude of females towards science is based on their view of science. Otto then described a variety of factors that may influence female attitudes over a wide range of ages.

Kumar (1991), observed significant difference between the mean scores of boys in the average effective group in respect of perception of teaching of science.

- There was no significant difference in attitude of boys and girls.
- Place of habitation did not have any impact on attitude towards science.
- Relation was established in relation to sex and places of habitations.

Dubey (1992), attempted to measure attitude towards science and concluded that whereas all groups of students showed attitude towards science, significant differences were observed between male and female science teachers.

Srivastava (1992), examined creativity among higher secondary students in relation to scientific aptitude and attitude towards science. Whereas the study showed relationship between scientific aptitudes and creativity, at the same time significant sex differences in aptitude, creativity and attitude towards science existed in her study.

Oppenheim (1992), studied on Questionnaire Design Interviewing and Attitude measurement and investigated what factors affect the success. For this reason, he examined students' attitudes towards science and found that Likert type attitude scales are appropriate to designing studies. Furthermore, Hendley (1995) found that it was very useful to obtain the opinion students' tendency to react towards science, which defined their beliefs, preference, decision, sensitive and thoughts. He found that girl students had lower positive attitudes toward science and are not successful in science.

Archer (1992), found that girls aged between 10 and 15 reported liking most strongly the three subjects regarded stereotypically as 'masculine' – mathematics, science and games. However, there was now some evidence beginning to appear that girls no longer hold such a stereotypical aversion to careers in science and were confident of their ability to undertake science courses (Colley *et al.,* 1994; Havard, 1996; Lightbody and Durnbell, 1996; Whitehead, 1996). Moreover, in terms of achievement in science, Elwood and Comber (1995) had shown that the situation had now reached a position, at least in the UK, where girls were doing as well, if not better than boys: What these figures (1994 GCSE results) showed was that in only one of these subjects, biology, were boys substantially ahead of girls, a subject for which girls had traditionally entered in large numbers to meet the requirement of taking a science subject. In all other eleven subjects girls were substantially ahead of boys in the proportion of A*–C grades obtained or else the gap was very narrow between the genders.

Watts and Bentley (1993), found that gender itself might only contribute a minor part in the attribution of success. Undoubtedly, the feminist perspective on this was that the very nature of science with its claims to universality and its non-reflexive, value free and objective nature, were inherently at odds with feminine values that value the human and affective aspects of knowledge (Harding, 1991; Keller, 1985).

Moon (1994), conducted a study on the relationship among gender, computer-experience and attitude towards computers and concluded that word-processing experience contributed to higher confidence levels and more positive attitudes to computers and these were culture free constructs.

Hendley, Parkinson, Stables and Tanner's (1995) study on gender difference in pupil attitudes to the national curriculum foundation subjects of English, mathematics, science and technology in key stage three in South Wales' education study of 4023 showed that, out of four core subject—science, mathematics, English and technology, science is least popular. This view of science is confirmed by a smaller scale qualitative study based on interviews with 190 pupils (Hendley, Stables and Stables, 1996). When asked which three subjects they liked best, science was ranked fifth out of nine subjects. However, this contrasts strongly with the response to the question "which three subjects do you like least"? Hence science emerged as the most disliked subject and interestingly least preferred by boys. Hendley *et al.* (1995) concluded that science is a 'love–hate' subject that elicits strong feelings in pupils.

Gardner (1995), commented that gender is the most significant factors and variable related towards pupils' attitude towards science. This view was supported by Schibeci (1984); Becker (1989) and Weinburgh (1995). In these studies boys had shown consistently more positive attitude to school science than girls, although this effect was stronger in Physics than in Biology.

Whitehead's (1996), research had attempted to explore in more detail the influence of gender stereotyping on choice. She found that, although there were significant gender distinctions within pupils' perceptions of subjects, these were not significant influences on subject choice. Girls doing mainly 'feminine' subjects, who were the focus of her study, described themselves as high on the stereotypical masculine trait of competence and were highly intrinsically motivated. Boys in contrast, taking mainly 'masculine' subjects, were more likely to be extrinsically motivated for status, recognition and a highly paid job describing themselves as high on the traits of competence and aggression. In general, boys were more likely to choose sex-stereotyped careers and she suggested that this reflected a greater need to establish and strengthen their gender identity than that of girls. Hence, she suggested that it was not, therefore, that girls were under-represented in mathematics and the physical sciences, but that boys were greatly over-represented; similarly, in languages, girls appeared to be over-represented in these areas only because the boys were so under-represented in them. Furthermore, she commented that if boys were choosing sex-appropriate subjects in order to conform to traditional notions of masculinity, then this was clearly undesirable both from the point of view of the individual, who might not necessarily be choosing those subjects at which they were most successful and for society as a whole, as it was unlikely to gain good scientists by such a process of choice. Such findings would also explain why boys in boys-only schools choose more arts and humanities courses as they are under less pressure to establish and conform to their gender identity.

Lightbody and Durnbell (1996), in a recent study in one school, using a slightly more sophisticated preferences ranking system, have shown that boys were far more likely to report liking than girls–a finding given additional salience by the work of Jovanoic and King (1998), which suggests that one of the major factors in girls antipathy towards science is their perception that they are better at other subjects.

Budhdev (1996), conducted a study of attitudes of secondary school students towards science and found that all the students exhibited positive attitude towards science and the attitude of boys towards science was more positive than girls.

Boone (1997), conducted a study on attitude towards science of selected middle school students in China. A preliminary investigation of similarities and differences as a function of gender and found that the girls selected strongly disagree in much larger percentages than the boys. It is also important to note that the responses of the girls to the seven significant items were ones in which girls were adamant in a supportive way towards science.

Woodward and Woodward (1998), conducted a research on girls and science and found that girls showed a higher preference than boys for health education, although the reverse was true for electricity. He further concluded that girls shown more attitude towards science than boys.

Fielding (1998), studied that girl's examination performance in science at age 16 indicated exceptional ability, why they chose not to study science further. Without exception, all of them indicated that they did not choose to pursue further study in science as it would limit their vocational choices to scientific careers—none of which they saw as appealing.

Johnston *et.al* (1999), conducted a research on the teaching and learning of primary science and found that girls were significantly more positive attitude towards science than boys and girls were more positive than boys about doing science in the classroom.

Stephens and Creaser (1999), studied on Information Science students, Information Technology experience and attitude towards computer science and found that males were found to have a significantly more positive attitude towards computer science than females. There were no differences between the intake years, not between the two age groups and no interactions between them. There was an interaction between year of study and age group in attitudes towards science. The attitudes of school leavers became more negative over time, whereas there was no pattern for the more mature students, although they reported significantly more positive attitudes in 1999 than in any previous year. Mature students were significantly more confident in class than school leavers, as might be expected.

Orhun and Orhun (2001), in the investigation of relation between attitude towards mathematics and attitude towards science of IX grade students in Eskiehir science high school according to some variables.

Their applying Likert type scales of attitude towards mathematics and science to IX grade student in Eskisehir science high school investigated the relation between them. It is investigated whether this relation changes according to academically successes and genders of these students or not. In this research, the positive relation was found between attitude towards mathematics and science. It is observed that this relation is on meaningful level according to academic success in girl and boy students, the graph of attitude towards mathematics versus attitude towards science in girl and boy students, the relation between them were investigated. It was observed that there existed significant relationship between them.

Lalitha and Lakshminarayan (2002), conducted a study of Attitude of +2 students towards physics laboratory work and found that achievement of +2 students in practical is a definite indicator of their achievement in theory, whereas their attitudes towards laboratory work is not considered to be a predictor of their achievement in theory. It may be concluded that the achievement of students in theory is independent of their attitudes towards laboratory work. The attitudinal factors that influence students are; laboratory work as an essential part of physics learning experience and more practical work than teachers' lectures. Age of the students had no influence on students' attitude towards laboratory work and their achievement in theory. Age differences are evident in achievement in practical. Male and female students did differ in their attitudes towards laboratory work and in their achievement in both theory and practical.

Gautam (2002), conducted a study of attitude towards science in relation to interest in science and found that girls exhibited greater attitude towards science than boys. Attitude towards science was positively related to interest in science. There was difference in attitude towards science of students with high, low and average interest in science. Students with high level interest in science exhibited superior attitudes towards science than their counterparts with low level interest in science.

Vidyapati and Rao (2003), studied on gender and socio-cultural differences in attitude towards science, creative ability and science achievement of ninth grades of Jawahar Navodaya Vidyalayas (JNVs), Mundali and found that there exists a significant gender difference in favour of girls in science achievement. Apart from this, no significant gender difference in attitude towards science, scientific creative abilities and no significant socio-cultural differences in attitude towards science, scientific creative abilities and science achievement have been observed.

Zimmerman (2004), conducted a research to study the secondary students' attitude towards mathematics. The purpose of the study was to investigate the attitude of secondary school students towards mathematics study and to compare the attitude of students in the USA with eight other countries and to compare differences in attitudes by gender for students in USA. The study also analysed the relationships between these attitudes and other mathematics learning factors and reported their impact on mathematics achievement.

Guzel (2004), studied the relationship between students' success in physics lessons and their attitude towards mathematics and found that female students show more positive attitude towards mathematic than male students. From the results he found that there is a close relationship between the students' attitudes towards mathematics and the achievements in physics and mathematics courses. This relationship was as follows: the more their attitudes were, the more their achievements would be. It was concluded that especially the male students were more successful than female students in physics.

Suresh and Rajarajeswari (2005), studied the influence of simulated experiment on the knowledge and attitudes of higher secondary students towards Bio-technology and Genetic Engineering and the major findings were as follows:

- The higher secondary school students had a poor knowledge and attitude towards bio-technology and genetic engineering.
- Boys, girls and mixed students differed significantly in their knowledge and attitude.
- There was significant difference in knowledge and attitude towards bio-technology and genetic engineering between the experimental group and control group and there was significant difference in students' relative retention of learning in bio-technology and genetic engineering between experimental and control group.
- There was a significant change in their attitude towards bio-technology and genetic engineering after learning bio-technology and genetic engineering through both simulated experiments and traditional method of teaching.

Sharma (2008), studied on problem solving ability and attitude towards science as determinants of academic achievement of higher secondary students and concluded that all three variables achievement and problem-solving ability, achievement and attitude towards science, attitude towards science and problem-solving ability all are significantly correlated, but relationship is low in boys and not in girls.

Sharma (2010), studied on attitude of secondary school students towards science and its relationship with gender and educational aspiration and found a positive correlation between them.

2.2 Attitude Towards Science and Socio-economic Status

Ghosh (1990), conducted study of attitude towards science and aptitude of the students and determination if some determinants of attitude towards science. Major findings were:

- Urban students did not show better performance in the scientific aptitude than rural students.
- Boys did not possess more scientific aptitude than girls.
- Boys did not possess better scientific attitude than girls.
- There was a positive relation between scientific aptitude and scientific attitude, scientific aptitude and academic motivation and scientific attitude and academic motivation. Scores in the scientific aptitude tests could be predicted from the scores of scientific attitude, academic motivation and SES of parents through multiple regression equation.
- Students having high scientific attitude were superior to those having low scientific attitude with respect to their attitude towards science.
- Urban students belonging to the high SES group had more scientific aptitude than urban students belonging to low SES group.
- Rural students belonging to the high SES did not show better attitude towards science than rural students belonging to the low SES group.

Ghosh (1990), showed that whereas scientific aptitude was related to attitude towards science, there were no such significant differences in respect of sex, socio-economic status and place of work among the various groups.

Breakwell and Beardsell (1992), found that SES was negatively associated with attitude towards school science. Children from lower SES had more positive attitudes. Breakwell identified attitudes to science as being more critically dependent on the support of the mother. However, she pointed out, mothers might be unwittingly perpetuating their sons more than their daughters. However, this finding was contrary to earlier findings by McEwen, Curry, and Watson (1986) and by Brown (1976), and the role of social class remains unclear. Breakwell's study was interesting in that, somewhat exceptionally, it tried to develop a model to account for children's attitudes. Like other studies (Simpson and Oliver 1990), it found some evidence for a relationship between parental support and attitudes to science. Breakwell's research identified extra-curricular activities as being correlated with parental support, particularly that of the father. However, her findings were somewhat of a contradiction to those of Woolnough (1994) in that she found no correlation between attitudes toward science and involvement in extra-curricular activities, whereas Woolnough found that involvement in these was a significant factor in choosing to study science post-16. Further evidence for the value of science clubs is provided by Kingsland (1991). However, these findings were not necessarily in disagreement as Breakwell was studying 11–16 year olds ($n = 1800$), while Woolnough's study was with post-16 children who had passed the point of choice and where the value of such activities might be more consciously recognised.

2.3 Attitude Towards Science and Achievement

Cannon and Simpson (1990), conducted a study on relationships among attitude towards science, motivation and achievement of ability grouped, seventh-grade, life science students and found that attitude towards science were higher for both males and females at the beginning of the year.

Soyibo (1990), conducted a research on a comparison of selected Lagos students' attitudes to and performance on a biology test and found that students' positive attitude towards science correlate highly with their science achievement.

Simpson and Oliver (1990), conducted a study on Attitude towards science and achievement motivation profiles of male and female science students in grades six through ten and found that males had more positive attitudes toward science, but that females were more highly motivated to achieve in science than males.

Koballa (1990), studied on attitude and related concepts in science education and confirmed the existence of the attitude-behaviour link. It was also found that student's attitudes towards science and highly related to their achievement in science.

Engstrom and Noonan (1990), conducted a research on science achievement and attitudes in Swedish schools of grades three, four, seven, eight and nine and found that boys have high positive attitudes toward science than girls.

Shrigley (1990), argued that attitude and ability scores could be expected to correlate moderately. Likewise, the measures used in the TIMSS study, albeit somewhat unsophisticated, had found a consistent relationship between attitude and achievement (Beaton *et al.* 1996). Weinburgh's (1995) meta-analysis of the research suggests that there was only a moderate correlation between attitude towards science and achievement, although this correlation was stronger for high and low ability girls indicated that, for these groups, 'doing well' in science was closely linked with 'liking science'. Similar findings had appeared in the major study conducted by Simpson and Oliver (1990), by Jovanoic and King (1998) and by Osborne and Collins (2000).

Raghavan (1991), stressed the importance of concept-mapping in learning physical science. He showed the relationship between concept-mapping and other variables such as achievement, cognitive ability and attitude towards science.

Ponte, Matos, Guimaraes, Leal and Canavarro (1991), conducted a study on students' views and attitudes towards mathematics teaching and learning and found that the students of tenth grade had a general positive attitude towards mathematics but did not perceive major changes. The conceptions, attitudes and expectations of the students regarding mathematics and mathematics teaching have been considered to be very significant factors underlying their school experience and achievement (Borasi, 1990; Shoenfeld, 1985).

Lin (1992), conducted a research on Trend analysis and prediction of students' science attitude and achievement in Taiwan and found that students' attitudes towards science are highly related to their achievement in science.

A study by Khatoon (1998), was aimed at relating student's attitude to science and achievement in a study on "Minority student attitude towards science and their achievement; A comparative study." Other studies focus on the changes or difference in student's attitude to science as a consequence of education.

Dhinsa and Chung (2003), studied on attitude and achievement of Brunei science students. He reported that there were no gender difference in attitude towards and achievement in science of students in co-educational schools. Another factor that attributes to the students attitude towards science was their level of English proficiency. The students' proficiency of the English Language was not of a standard required to understand spoken and written English in their science classes. It was believed that students' difficulty in understanding and expressing themselves in English contributes to their low achievement in science.

Subrata (2007), conducted a study of academic achievement in mathematics in relation to cognitive style and attitude towards mathematics and he found that boys and girls differed significantly on all the three measures under consideration. Boys performed significantly better than their counterparts on all the variables. Boys showed more favourable attitude towards mathematics than the girls may be due to the tendency of not taking a logically harder subject by the girls with pleasure.

Chang (2008), conducted a study on science achievement and student's self-confidence and interest in science: A Taiwan representative sample study. He observed that there existed a strong relationship between science achievement and self-confidence, interest in science. Statistically significant correlation existed between student's attitude towards science and their SCIS with a moderate effect size; the correlation is even higher with almost larger effect size for a sub sample of higher SCIS and lower SCIS student. Result of t-test analysis also revealed that there were significant in student's attitude towards science and their knowledge (including physics, chemistry, biology and earth science subscales) and reasoning skill subtests scores between higher SCIS and lower SCIS students also suggested that both student's SCIS subscales significantly explain the variance of their science achievement and reasoning ability with large effect sizes.

2.4 Attitude Towards Science and Intelligence

Ahamed, Raheem and Hasan (2003), conducted a study on attitude of secondary school students towards science in relation to sex, socio-economic status and intelligence and the findings were:

- Both boys and girls showed equally positive attitude towards science;
- The students who are from high socio-economic background showed better positive attitude toward science than middle as well as lower level SES background students;
- The students with high intelligence showed more positive attitude towards science than middle as well as lower intelligence groups. The students from middle intelligence level also showed better positive attitude towards science than the lower one.

2.5 Attitude Towards Science and Classroom Climate

Talton and Simpson (1990), studied on Relationships of attitude towards self, family, and school with attitude towards science among adolescents. In that study, American students in grades 6-10 were evaluated. These authors comment that "the classroom environment variable predicted the greatest amount of variance in attitude towards science in all grades."

Simpson and Oliver (1990), drew a conclusion that school, particularly classroom variables, is the strongest influence on attitude towards science. They conducted extensive and major study in Carolina. Evidences that it is the quality of teaching of school science that is significant determinant of attitude towards school science has been found by Woolnough, whose research showed that it was a major factor in continuing with science education post-16. This finding is confirmed by Ebenezer and Zoller's (1993) study of grade 10 (age 15/16) student's attitudes towards science, both of whom found that the most important variable affecting students attitudes was the kind of science teaching they experienced.

Tobias (1990)'s study aimed to explore why so many college students turn away from science in the course of their degree studies and involved a group of post-graduates who had successfully completed their degrees in other subjects. For a fee, the group of surrogate students were willing to re-visit introductory courses in physics and chemistry in order to audit these for the research. They each enrolled for a particular course and participated in it, attending all the lectures and doing the homework assignments and examinations. They were asked to focus their attention on what might make introductory science 'hard' or even 'alienating' for students like themselves. The seven case studies in the report reveal some common problems with introductory courses that were found to be alienating; the courses focused on problem-solving techniques and lacked an intellectual overview of the subject; there were too many 'how much' questions, not enough discussion of 'how' or 'why'; pedagogy was condescending and patronising, examinations were not challenging; there was no community or discussion and the atmosphere was competitive. One student summed up the problem as 'the absence of history or context, "the tyranny of technique", the isolation of the learner and the struggle to attend in a sea of inattentiveness'. These research findings, then, provided strong confirmatory evidence for children's and adults' anecdotal stories about the influence of teachers on students' attitudes to school science and on subject choice. Furthermore, they raised substantial questions about why the pedagogy of some science teachers was so unappealing to the majority of students, suggested that, while science teachers might be knowledgeable about their subject, they were failing to achieve their primary task of establishing a range of varied learning opportunities and communicating their subject effectively.

Malviya (1991), attempted to study the attitude towards science and interest in science among school going adolescents. He found positive attitude towards science among all the students. There was significant difference in attitude with reference to locale. Attitude and different factors of interest were significantly correlated.

Nellaippan (1992), found strong relationship between learning environment and attitude towards science. There existed difference in attitude towards science and scientific interest in relation to sex, locale and learning environment.

Myers and Fouts (1992), conducted a study on 699 students from 27 high schools in America. It was found that the most positive attitude were associated with a high level of involvement, very high level of personal support, strong positive relationship with classmates, and the use of variety of teaching strategies and unusual learning activities. Similar evidence that variety is the spice of science education comes from the work of Piburn (1993) who, using data from interviews with 149 students reported that it is one of the key factors in generating interest in science education.

Bagchi (1993-94), studied the impact of different educational practices on student's attitude towards science, while Maitra and Maitra (1997) focused on a specific aspect of science that is exploring student's attitude towards laboratories and other related practical work in science.

Ebenezer and Zollar (1993), conducted a study on grade ten student's perceptions of the attitude towards science teaching and school science and found that "the most important variable that affected students' attitude towards science was the kind of science teaching that they experienced." The contradiction between student's interest in science and their liking for school science is also highlighted by the work of Ebenezer and Zollar (1993) where in the study in the US of 11564 grade 10 (16 years old) students, 72 per cent of the sample of students question indicated that they thought science to be valuable and 73 per cent opined that science in school is important, but nearly 40 per cent indicated that they found science classes boring. This speaks least attitude towards science education.

Stanisstreet (1993), studied on attitudes of children to the use of animals and found that students' knowledge of science is random and has no plan. One of the factors which affects attitude towards science negatively is abstraction increased in mathematics and the other is irregular and heterogeneous structure of the science classes. Besides, students' knowledge, environmental conclusions on their daily behaviours play role on the attitude towards science negatively.

Piburn and Baker (1993), found that students' point of view to the nature of the science change according to the educational materials. In the 10th and 11th grades of the high school, the positive attitudes towards science decrease.

Crawley and Koballa (1994), studied on attitude research in science education and found that students had less positive attitude towards science. He suggested to develop the positive attitude towards science, more contemporary and more persuasive hypothesis must be made.

Woolnough (1994), identified factors as contributing to such teaching included a supply of well-qualified, enthusiastic graduate science staff (including graduates in physics and engineering), who not only had a good spread of expertise across science, but who also had individual subject loyalty. Good teaching was characterised by teachers being enthusiastic about their subject, setting it in everyday contexts and running well-ordered and stimulating science lessons. Good teachers were also sympathetic and willing to spend time, both in and out of lessons, talking with the students about science, careers and individual problems. One implication of the introduction of national or standards-based curricula, suggests Woolnough, had been the tendency to restrict and de-skill the good science teacher, with the loss of those 'extra bits', in particular extra-curricular activities that contribute to good science teaching. One of Woolnough's recommendations for preserving good science teaching was that teachers should teach what they feel comfortable with, as teachers in the study were happiest and most enthusiastic teaching their specialist subjects – a finding that clearly had implications for the organisation of the curriculum in separate versus integrated disciplines.

Defiana (1995), conducted a study on environmental awareness and relating current issues to biology and found that using integrated science environment activities improved high school students' attitude towards science and awareness about the environment.

Shamai (1996), conducted a research on elementary school students' attitudes toward science and their course of studies in high school and found that there was almost no relationship between the different attitudes toward science and other school subjects in grade six and course of study in grade eleven. The only exception is girls' attitudes toward computer studies in grade six.

Havard's (1996), work suggested that the problem lied with physics, as over 50 per cent of his sample indicated that they did not enjoy the subject at all, or very little, whereas over 60 per cent enjoyed biology a lot or quite a lot. One factor might be that physics was often taught by teachers who lack specialist knowledge and who had little enthusiasm for the subject. In such situations, teachers who lack confidence and familiarity fall back on didactic modes of teaching and the quality of teaching and learning was impoverished. For instance, in England, surveys indicate that there was within the science teaching community a considerable imbalance in the subject specialisms of 'science teachers' that was weighted heavily towards a specialisation in Biology (Dillon, Osborne, Fairbrother, and Kurina, 2000). Moreover, such candidates are normally significantly better qualified and of a higher calibre. The consequence was that biology, wherever it was taught, was more likely to be taught by a specialist with enthusiasm and interest and, as we (Osborne and Simon, 1996) and other workers (Shulman, 1986; Turner-Bisset, 1999) had shown, teacher subject knowledge was a determinant of effective teaching. As Tobin and Fraser (1988), in their study of American teachers point out: because teachers did not have the content knowledge, errors of fact were made and opportunities to elaborate on student understandings and to diagnose misunderstandings were missed. In some instances, flaws were evident in attempts to explain concepts with which students were having difficulty and in other cases, analogies were selected which compounded student problems in understanding concepts. The net result of teachers' lack of content knowledge in high school classes was an emphasis on learning of facts and a sewing of seeds for the development or reinforcement of misconceptions. This argument would also explain Woolnough's (1994) and Sharp *et al.*'s (1996) findings that separate subjects were more successful at engendering interest and take-up of physical science at A-level as they would have predominantly been taught by subject specialists.

Cooper and McIntyre (1996), found that there were common aspects of teaching that were perceived to be effective by both teachers and pupils. These were: clear goals for pupil learning; clarity of communication of lesson goals and agenda to pupils; use of preview and review of lesson content; helping students to contextualise content in terms of their own experience and knowledge, as well as in terms of other teaching goals and learning experiences; some willingness to allow pupils to have input into goal and agenda setting; a supportive social context designed by the teacher to help pupils feel accepted, cared for and valued; an ability and willingness to allow for different cognitive styles and ways of engaging with the learning process among pupils, through multiple examplification, and the use of different types of illustration and mode of presentation, and offering pupils a choice from a menu of possible ways of engaging; and a willingness to take into account pupil circumstances and to modify/pace/structure learning tasks accordingly.

Vidhate (1997), conducted a study on preparation of the teaching programme for development of attitude towards science based on standard VIII science syllabus and a study of the effectiveness of programme and such programmes were aimed at improving students' attitude towards science.

Attempts were made in a few studies to identify the factors related to attitude and science such as the doctoral work by Rani (1997) entitled "A study of problems of science education and attitude of students towards science in high school of East Khasi Hills district, Meghalaya".

Sandhu (1998), tried to ascertain the school and non-school factors as determinant of attitude towards science. A standard measure of scientific temper was developed by Sharma and Shukla (1999) "CSAT as a diagnostic measure of scientific temper". All these studies amply justify that enough researches have been conducted in this area.

Jayasree (1998), studied on socialisation ability, scientific attitude and attitude towards science in junior college students and established a relationship between scientific attitude and attitude towards science.

Lin (1998), conducted a study on enhancing college students' attitudes toward science through the history of science and found that the teaching of historical cases in chemistry made a significant contribution to the students' positive change of attitudes towards science.

Fraser (1998), conducted a research on science learning environments and found that the quality of the science classroom environment was important to attitudinal outcomes in science, they also shown that the quality of assessment tasks was linked positively to attitudinal outcomes.

Reiss (1999) studied on students' attitude towards science: A long-term perspective and he found that students develop attitude to science, in part, as a result of their developing attitude to school science lessons. Attitudes to school science were affected by what the content was, how the subject was taught, and how it was assessed. The findings also helped to shed light on the reasons why many students lose interest in science during the course of their secondary science education.

Osborne and Collins (2000), concluded that the single most important change that could be made to improve the quality of science education would be the recruitment *and retention* of able, bright enthusiastic teachers of science.

Barton (2000), studied on Crafting Multi-cultured Science Education with Pre-service Teachers Through Service-Learning and found that the teaching method, the support of the structure of the school and the family, students' attitude towards the school affect the attitude toward science too. Usually, the way that science is represented in the classroom and perceived by students, even when teachers believe they are presenting it in authentic and context dependent ways tends to alienate many students from science.

Bricheno (2000), conducted a research on attitude towards science changes on transition and cited the importance of small group practical work in promoting positive attitude towards science.

Telli, Rakici and Cakiroglu (2000), conducted a study on learning environment and students' attitudes towards biology and found that high school students had favourable perceptions of their learning environment in biology classrooms. They also perceived that they had greater student cohesiveness and task orientation. Gender was found to be a significant factor that differentiates students' perceptions of biology learning environments.

Campbell (2001), studied on children' perceptions of science education at primary and secondary school and cited the importance of small group practical work in promoting positive attitude towards science. He also found that, when asked about what they liked best in science, primary children most frequently replied 'doing experiments' and 'finding out new things'.

Ponchaud (2001), conducted a research on primary science and found that children liked best 'doing experiments' in science. The reasons given included that doing experiments was fun, that they found out things and that they were learning whilst enjoying themselves. They have reported on the importance of experimental work both for motivating children and enhancing their attitude towards science.

Sulekha (2002), conducted a study to find out relationship between attitude towards science and learning environment and found that formality, facilitation, goal direction, competition, involvement conformity and diversity in the classroom were associated with attitude towards science. Cohesiveness, friction, favouritism, difficulty, apathy, democracy, cliqueness, disorganisation, creative stimulation encouragement and speed in the classroom were not associated with attitude towards science. There were no gender differences in the attitude of students towards science.

Dorman (2002), conducted a research on classroom environment, academic efficacy and attitude towards science and found that there were positive associations between classroom environment dimensions and attitude towards science. He also reported significant positive correlations between academic efficacy and Teacher Support, Involvement, Investigation, Task Orientation and Equity.

Osman and Halim (2002), conducted research on anchoring science education towards scientifically literate Malaysian Society and found that students' attitude towards science was high and there existed significant difference in terms of students' attitude towards science with respect to level of educational experiences.

Regan and Childs (2003), found that Ireland's student participation in the sciences at leaving certificate (LC) level has fallen considerably in the last fifteen years. They evaluated the opinion and attitude of students at junior certificate to science, prior to LC subject choice, as part of an intervention strategy to promote chemistry. This article is concerned with the reasons given by a group of third year students for their like or dislike of the science and their reason for choosing to study chemistry in future. This case study shows positive views of science; most students would voluntarily choose science and chemistry (in the future) because they find it interesting. Physics was perceived to be less interesting than chemistry.

Dunlop and Catherine (2004), studied on the perceptions of the learning environment, attitude towards science and understandings of the nature of science among prospective elementary teachers in an innovative science course and found that there exists strong relationship between the learning environment and attitude towards science. Associations between the learning environment and the student outcomes of attitude towards science and understandings of the nature of science were explored.

Fisher and Koul (2004), conducted a study on students' perception of science learning environment in Jammu: Attitudes and gender differences. He found that all the seven scales of WIHIC (What is Happening in this Class?) questionnaire viz. student cohesiveness, teacher support, involvement, Investigation, Task orientation, Cooperation and Equity Correlated significantly with attitude towards science classroom environment. The Investigation, Task orientation and Equity scales were found to be independent predictors of individual students' attitude towards science lessons. The girls had significantly higher score than the boys on cohesiveness, Task orientation, Cooperation and Equity scales of WIHIC.

Alwis (2004), conducted a study on attitude towards learning science in English: A case study of schools in Kota Samarahan and found that students with good attitude towards English also have a positive attitude towards learning science in English. It was found that in general, attitude towards science is good. Female students have better attitude towards science in general.

Thabor (2004), conducted a study on creative thinking ability and attitude towards science among students of secondary schools having different organisational climates and the findings were as follows:

- There existed significant difference in attitude towards science among students belonging to schools of different types of management.
- There existed significant difference in attitude towards science among students of classes VIII, IX and X.
- There existed significant difference in attitude towards science among students belonging to schools with different organisational climates.
- There was no significant difference in attitude towards science between students of rural and urban secondary schools.

- Non-tribal secondary school students exhibited significantly more favourable attitude towards science than tribal secondary school students.

Karthikeyan and Mohideen (2005), conducted a study of correlation between the availability and utilisation of science laboratory facilities in higher secondary schools and attitude of higher secondary students towards science practical and the major findings were as follows:

- It was found that there was positive correlation between the availability and utilisation of science laboratory facilities and students attitude towards science practical.
- The attitude to the higher secondary students in girls' schools and the government schools were more positive than boys and co-education schools and aided and self-finance schools respectively.
- Mother played a vital role in developing students' attitude towards science practical.

Dorman, Fisher, Waldrip (2007), conducted a study on students' perceptions of learning environments and assessment with academic efficacy and attitude towards science in Australian Secondary Schools and found that classroom environment and student perceptions of assessment were significant positive predictors of attitude towards science and academic efficacy.

Askwall and Hermanson (2007), conducted a study on young people's attitudes towards science and researchers and concluded that in Sweden, young people seem to be more skeptical of scientific and technological developments than adults, whereas the opposite is true in many other countries. They also found that young people had less "respect" for research and science than older people. They also had less confidence in researchers.

Adesoji (2008), while conducting a study on managing student's attitude towards science through problem-solving instructional strategy designed to further clarify the claim by several author that methods of instruction could change student's attitude positively towards science. It was the belief of the author that if students were allowed to develop higher cognitive processes through problem-solving strategies, either as teacher directed or self-directed, their attitude towards chemistry might change positively. Therefore the effect of teacher directed and self-directed problem-solving strategies on student attitude towards chemistry was investigated. The finding in this study showed that students in the experimental group developed more positive attitude towards chemistry after the treatment. It was then recommended that teachers should adopt problem-solving strategies in their teaching in order to win many more students to chemistry. Besides giving students the content, the process is equally important for them to comprehend some scientific concepts and principles. This could make them develop more positive attitude towards the learning of science.

2.6 Attitude Towards Science and Management

Mordi (1991), studied on factors associated with pupils' attitude towards science in Nigerian Primary Schools. He evaluated attitude towards science of Nigerian sixth graders and tried to correlate those attitudes to other factors. One of the conclusions of the study was that attitude towards science seems to be primarily due to school experiences.

Chauhan (2008), studied on attitude of secondary school students towards science and found that there was no significant difference in attitude towards science of secondary school students in relation to sex. There existed significant difference in attitude towards science of secondary school students in relation to the students' parental education. Students whose father's educational status was high were possessed better positive attitude towards science. She found that students of non-government schools had high attitude towards science than students of government schools. She also found that students from urban background had high positive attitude towards science than students from rural background.

Ravana, Mary and Julie (2008), conducted a study on attitude towards mathematics of XI standard students of Trichy District. They found that there is no significant difference in the attitude owing to differences in their gender, religion and medium of instruction. There is significant difference in attitude owing to differences in their stream of study, types of schools management and socio-economic status.

Lama (2010), conducted a study on achievement in science in relation to attitude towards science at the secondary level and found that students having high level of attitude towards science exhibited higher academic achievement in science compared to their counterparts of low attitude and low achievement. He also found that there existed significant difference in attitude towards science and achievement in science of secondary school students in relation to sex and type of management.

Mishra (2011), conducted a study on the relationship between reasoning ability in and attitude towards science of the students at the secondary level and found a significant relationship between them. She also found that there existed significant difference in attitude towards science of students due to sex and management.

2.7 Attitude Towards Science and Other Variables

Whitfield (1980), argued that the rejection of science was accounted for by the perception that it was a difficult subject but his findings, based on data collected in the 1970s, now lack significance because of the considerable changes that have occurred in the science curriculum (in particular, the move to balanced or integrated science) since his study was conducted. The work of Osborne and Collins (2000) would suggest that, for many, the contemporary curriculum may suffer from the obverse problem with too much emphasis on undemanding activities such as recall, copying and a lack of intellectual challenge. Perhaps surprisingly, Whitfield's type of study had not been repeated on a large scale. However, a recent study by Lightbody and Durnbell (1996) in one school, using a slightly more sophisticated preference ranking system, had shown that boys were far more likely to report liking science than girls--a finding given additional salience by the work of Jovanoic and King (1998), which suggested that one of the major factors in girls' antipathy towards science was their perception that they were better at other subjects. Preference ranking was simple to use and the results of such research were easily presented and interpreted. Its fundamental problem was that it was a relative scale. Hence, it was possible for a student with an extremely positive attitude to all school subjects to still rank science as the least popular and yet still had a much more favourable attitude than another student who had a strong dislike for all subjects and ranks science first. Neither was it suitable for the measurement of attitude change as its blunt nature might not expose changes in attitudes as a student's attitude to other subjects might change as well. However, this would suggest that it was an instrument not to be used in isolation rather than discarded totally.

The simple nature of this technique still provides an effective answer to the question that was essentially that asked by teachers and schools—'How popular was science compared to other subjects?' It was therefore surprising that such surveys had not been repeated more often.

Kahneman and Tversky (1984), provided some insight into the effect of such perceptions on subject choice at the point of choice. Their study found that when the negative aspects of a course of action were emphasised, people preferred to risk the choice that leads to the definite avoidance of *loss* rather than risk an opportunity that may have *no loss* whatsoever. Thus, school students confronted with a choice that is high risk, although potentially with high financial gain (i.e., doing science with its concomitant risk of failure) and one of lower risk (i.e., the greater certainty of success with arts-based courses), will choose the low-risk option even though the financial rewards may be less.

Taylor (1993), and Modood (1993), conducted study on cultural attitudes towards the study of science and found that, compared with their white peers, Asian students had a clear preference to study for degrees in medicine-related studies, engineering or mathematics. Moreover, a disproportionately low percentage applied to become teachers. In contrast, Afro-Caribbean students seem to shy away from science preferring to pursue degrees in the social sciences. More recent American research with over 1000 students in Grade three, Grade six, Grade eight and Grade ten also showed a similar picture, indicating that ethnic origin was significantly associated with attitudes towards science and a career in science (Greenfield, 1995). Caucasians were found to have the most positive attitudes towards science and Japanese-Americans were most positively inclined towards scientific careers. In this research, the influence of ethnic origin was found to be more significant than gender.

Simpson, Koballa, Oliver, and Crawley (1994), found that science classrooms had influenced on students' attitudes of new, as compared with traditional, curriculum materials or instructional techniques. Most of these studies had been conducted in the US and, apart from a major study focusing on Harvard Project Physics, had been small-scale enquiries. The results had not been conclusive. As Gardner (1975) commented, 'in most cases, a particular treatment group's mean attitudes have been shifted a fraction of a standard deviation along the attitude continuum' providing little, if any, meaningful information.

Woolnough (1994), found that for a small minority of academic pupils (usually boys), interest and enthusiasm for science was stimulated by the challenge presented by the abstract and mathematical aspects of science, particularly physics, and the desire to explore the subject in more depth. The evidence todate would suggest that, since the fundamental nature of the problem was negative attitudes towards school science, useful insights could be obtained by *focused studies* of classrooms where *effective teaching of science*, as judged by students, was to be found. For the research evidence shows clearly that it is the teacher variables that are the most significant factor determining attitude, not curriculum variables.

Cheng *et al.* (1995), found that the most significant factors correlating with uptake of physical sciences were the grades achieved at GCSE in science and mathematics. This suggested that science was only taken by students who did well and not as an incidental or additional subject. Whether this was a self-imposed restriction or a selection criterion imposed by schools was essentially irrelevant – the fact that only able pupils did physical sciences reinforced the notion that it was for the intelligent and therefore difficult. Was it possible, therefore, that physical sciences now had a similar image in students' minds to that associated with Greek in the 1960s – a subject that was only done by the very able or the slightly eccentric?

Woodrow (1996), argued that research on pupil life stories showed that Asian parents had a particularly important effect on student career choice. Within Asian families, career decisions will generally tend to favour longer term advantages compared with the more individualistic and immediately attractive choices made by students within contemporary Caucasian cultures in which personal enjoyment and/or perceived ability might play a more significant element. Moreover, within mainstream English society, the valuing of professions above trade was deep seated, reinforced by the financial disparities between arts-related careers and the sciences, and a nineteenth century disdain for anything that was not rooted in the classics or Christianity (Barnett, 2001). Some antipathy to science was shown by one of Breakwell and Beardsell's (1992) findings that a negative attitude to science was correlated with pupils coming from middle-class families. However, if science-based careers were less economically profitable, why were they the predominant choice with the Asian community? As Woodrow points out, all the research had done so far was shown that different groups hold different perspectives on the value of science-based careers and possibly science itself.

Havard (1996), found that chemistry was less appealing than physics. Some measure of attitudes towards school science can be obtained by asking pupils to rank their liking of school subjects, which has been the approach taken by Whitfield (1980) and Ormerod

(1971). Their relative popularity then gives some indication of students' attitudes towards the subject. Whitfield's analysis of 1971 IEA data for English students provided a graphic illustration that physics and chemistry were two of the least popular subjects post-14 and that these were distanced in pupils' minds from biology, a finding noted also by Ormerod and Duckworth (1975) and confirmed as still extant in a small but significant study by Osborne and Collins (2000). The latter study was innovative in its use of focus groups to explore 16-year-old student's views and attitudes towards science in depth.

Lemke (2001), argued from a socio-cultural perspective that contemporary science was a product of European cultures, and a middle-class subculture at that. For those who lie outside the orbit of such cultures by virtue of their ethnic origin or social status, the nature of what counts as knowledge and what counts as explanation might be startlingly different. Changing students' minds, therefore, requires more than their assent to the bare facts, logical structure and epistemology of Western science. For it demands, in addition, a felt commitment, a bond with a community and a change in identity that, some would argue, is equivalent to a cultural border crossing (Aikenhead, 1995). The implication drawn by Lemke was that it was no longer tenable to imagine that engaging with science was an equivalent process for all demanding only logical thought and application, and that, rather, cultural and class difference might be a significant aspect of many pupils' attitudes towards science.

2.8 Major Findings of the Reviews

From the reviews the following conclusions were made:

(i) Components of attitude towards science were intellectual honesty, open mindedness, habit of criticism, habit of suspended judgement, objectivity, aversion to superstition, rational outlook, etc.

(ii) Gender difference in attitude towards science was not very much significant at the secondary level. Hence the benefits of science and the awareness about gender parity in society motivated the parents to send both sons and daughters for science education.

(iii) Socio-economic status as a strong determinant of developing positive attitude towards science. The parents of higher SES groups have sound educational and financial background that was well-known about market forces. Therefore their children were motivated to read science.

(iv) Science attitude is having a strong relationship with scientific reasoning, achievement motivation and intelligence.

(v) The students with high intelligence showed more positive attitude towards science than middle as well as lower intelligence groups. The students from middle intelligence level also showed better positive attitude towards science than the lower one.

(vi) There existed significant difference in attitude towards science among students belonging to schools of different types of management. Higher level of involvement is necessary for the development of attitude towards science.

(vii) Effective classroom teaching is also a predictor to development of attitude towards science.

3

Attitude Towards Science: Methodology

3.1 Introduction

The purpose of study was to measure attitude towards science in relation to types of schools, types of management, school environment for studying science, school success, gender, father's educational status, mother's educational status and intelligence variations. Therefore it was an *ex-post-facto* study for the fact that attitude towards science and other variables were studied as they were. Here the design was a normative survey study of descriptive design where attitude towards science had been studied in relation to the above mentioned intervening variables.

3.2 The Sample

The sample for the investigation comprised 400 boys and girls drawn from two types of management in government schools and non-government schools from Cuttack and Bhubaneswar cities on simple random basis. The procedure adopted for the sampling design has been described hereunder. The simple random sampling procedure had been adopted for the investigation.

There are many techniques of sampling. This investigator adopted the techniques of simple random sampling, since the type of schools selected for study can be classified on the basis of their nature of management, composition of student population, girls' schools, boys' schools and co-education schools, school success (high achieving schools and low achieving schools) and school environmental conditions.

The details of the sampling procedures have been described in the following few lines. The selection of 18 schools from a total school of 180 had been done in such a manner that every unit of the population had an equal chance of being chosen and selection of anyone unit in no way is tied to the selection of any other. The law of chance was allowed to operate freely in selection of such a sample.

For the present study for selecting 18 schools at random from a serially numbered population of 180 schools of Cuttack and Bhubaneswar city, the investigator had used a table of random numbers. From the table of random numbers, therefore researcher selected a number having three digits. So the first 18 numbers from the same column of random numbers starting with 399 had been written down. After writing down the number the first three digits from the table of random numbers 43 numbers were deleted because they were larger than the population of 180 described. And the numbers so selected were considered from the stand point of a number less than 180.

After selecting the same earmarked 18 schools categorisation had been made under the independent variables of gender, type of schools and type of management. Then the sample had been collected as per the independent variables of socio-economic status, school environment condition and school success.

3.3 Tools Used

The tools used for this study were:

- Mishra's (2008) scale to measure Attitude towards Science. This scale had been developed by the investigator.
- Group test of General Mental Ability by Jalota (1951) had been used for assessing intelligence.
- Socio Economic Status Scale of Nayak (2005) had been used to determine the socio economic background of students.
- Information Schedule on School Environmental Condition (ISSEC) developed by Parida (1994) had been used to assess school environment climate.

3.3.1 Mishra's (2008) Scale to Measure Attitude Towards Science

The above attitude scale for scientific attitude was developed by investigator (2008). This scale was meant for secondary school students. The scale consisted of 75 statements under five point scale. The scale was constructed on the lines of Likert having five options mainly, SA, A, U, D and SD. The respondent was required to encircle the letter to which he agreed the most. The scale consisted of both positive and negative statements. In case of the positive statements the marks were 5, 4, 3, 2 and 1 respectively and in case of negative statements the marks were just reverse such as 1, 2, 3, 4 and 5.

The validity of the test was calculated by validating the same with another attitude scale. Therefore concurrent validity was 0.958. The reliability of the scale was measured by split half and was found to be 0.89 which were significant at 0.01 level of significance. The test was standardised over class IX student of Orissa consisting of samples from C.B.S.E., I.C.S.E. and State Board of Secondary Education.

3.3.2 Group Test of General Mental Ability by Jalota (1951)

This was a test of General Mental Ability. It was a 25 minutes test. There were five pages of this test with 100 questions. Examples of various types of problems were set in this test. All questions were in simple language. In each case alternative answers were given and were asked simply to choose the right answer and write its number on the answer sheet. There was only one correct answer to each question and each correct answer carried one mark.

The Test paper was tried for 25 minutes only. Another 20 minutes were usually required for seating the candidates, the distribution of the test answer sheet, the explanation of examples and the later collection of the test materials. An investigator with the help of two assistants can easily test a group of 20-25 students. About four helpers were required to deal with a larger batch of about 40 candidates.

3.3.3 Socio-economic Status Scale of Nayak (2005)

The socio-economic status scale of Nayak (2005) had been adopted to study socio-economic status of the parents of the children. The scale constituted of three parts education, occupation and income. Each of these categories had nine sub-categories. The total score of sub-categories checked in each criterion show the socio-economic status of the subject. The scale was standardised over the population of Orissa, secondary schools of Cuttack, Puri and Bhubaneswar.

The validity and reliability of the scale was determined where the retest reliability co-efficient was found to be 0.87, concurrent validity co-efficient is 0.61 and inter-rater reliability index was 0.93.

3.3.4 Information Schedule on School Environmental Condition (ISSEC) Developed by Parida (1994)

It was in the form of a booklet and consists of five pages. The schedule consisted of 103 statements belonging to the different components of the school climate described below. The items were distributed over three inputs or subtests, namely, Teacher Input, Material Input and Process Input.

The teacher input consisted of items like the numbers of teachers, their academic qualifications, professional qualifications, length of teaching experience of the principals and the teachers, in-service training programmes and participation in different co-curricular activities.

Under the material input items like the nature of the school building (kutcha, pucca or asbestos rooms), area provision for teaching, gardening, playing, toilets, indoor games, parking facilities, common room for teachers and students, availability of teaching aids for different academic subjects like the availability of audio aids, visual aids, audio-visual aids, library facilities and the laboratory facilities were included.

Under the process input items like the methods of instruction, methods of pupil evaluation, reporting performance of the students, organisation of educational tours, debates, workshops, exhibitions, essay competitions, talent search competitions, creative writing, model exhibition, projects, utilisation of school television programme and the facilities for school aquarium were included.

The total score of the school was obtained by summation of the scores allotted according to the scoring manual. So far as the validity and the reliability were concerned, reliability had been found to be 0.74 by

Kuder Richardson Method. The validity of the scale was found to be 0.54 which was highly significant.

3.4 Development of the Scale (Attitude towards Science)

The term attitude begins as a relatively simple one-dimensional concept consisting of the affective component of psychological object and has grown into a complex multi-dimensional concept consisting of the three domains of experience, cognitive, affective and conative. Attitudes are ethics. How one is disposed towards a particular thing, place or a person reflects one's attitudes. An attitude is hence a condition of mind that brings in imagination and emotional states which are the outcome of previous experience. Aiken (2002) gave his views on attitude as an opinion which can be regarded as the overt, conscious, verbal demonstration. Opinions are less central, more specific, more changeable and more factually based than attitudes. Opinions are expressed in words but attitudes may not be. A belief is a conviction, that something is true, even though it cannot be rigorously proved. A belief is in between, somewhere is knowledge and attitude.

Gregory (2005) gave a positive definition of attitude. According to him "Attitudes may be viewed as learned cognitive, affective and behavioural pre-dispositions to respond positively or negatively to certain objects, situations, institutions, concepts or persons".

The central constituent of attitudes is that they always have an evaluative component to them involving positive or negative responses of same kind. Attitudes serve motivational functions by helping individuals organise their perceptions and make sense out of the world. They condition behaviour. So an unfavourable attitude will cause a reaction either of avoidance or of aggression. A neutral attitude develops indifference and a favourable attitude develops a seeking behaviour. Attitudes range by degrees from one extreme to other and the use of the terms favourable, indifference or unfavourable is merely for convenience. An attitude is an observable, hypothetical construct. Moore (1970) has operationally defined attitude towards science as an opinion or position taken with respect to a psychological object in the field of science. Attitudes condition behaviour and therefore are of paramount importance in education. It is one of the fundamental responsibilities of the educationists to develop positive attitudes among students towards socially desirable goals. In order to assess the degree of change that is occurring in the attitude of students it is essential that some standardised tools be prepared. Without such instruments it won't be possible to carry out any worthwhile research in attitudinal changes. Such tools will be of great use not only to educationists but also to the social agents, psychologists and administrators.

Under the new curriculum science is a compulsory subject up to high school stage. One of the objectives of teaching science is to inculcate attitude towards science among the pupils because scientific attitudes are the most important outcomes of science teaching. Attitude towards science is viewed in terms of critical in observation and thought, open mindedness, curiosity to learn, objectivity in approach, unbiased and impartial judgement, belief in truth etc. It is defined in the book "Rethinking Science Education" that open mindedness, a desire for accurate knowledge, confidence in procedures for seeking knowledge and the expectation that the solution of the problem will come through the use of verified knowledge all relate to attitude towards science. Indicators of attitudes are more generalised aspects of behaviour than are process skills.

The purpose of this scale would be to know whether or not the students have developed favourable attitudes towards science as a discipline. The underlying assumption being that one of the outcomes of science education is the development of positive attitude towards the subject. In India, there is a lack of standardised scales on attitude towards science which may be available commercially for use by the teachers and research workers. Hence, it was thought relevant to develop a dependable attitude scale for measuring the attitude of students towards science.

3.4.1 Planning for the Development of the Scale

For development of the scale, the first step was planning which comprises selection of content, adequacy in representation of the context under coverage of content matter, favourableness and unfavourableness dimensions, number of items, format of attitude scale construction, time period required for administration etc., were considered. The techniques of attitude scale construction also come under the planning stage. Which technique would be most appropriate for assessing attitude towards science of secondary school students wise given due consideration. The details of these procedures are described hereunder.

3.4.2 Selection of Content

The contents to be covered under the attitude towards science were selected from literature reviews on development of attitude scales towards science. The following scales were reviewed thoroughly.

- Science Attitude Scale (SAS) of Grewal (1990)
- Attitude Towards Science Scale by Kar (1990)
- Scientific Attitude Scale by Bhagwat (2006)
- Scientific Attitude Scale by Gakhar and Kaur (2004)

- Attitude Towards Science and Scientists by Sood (1975)

In the book "Rethinking Science Education" by Henry (1960) open mindedness, a desire for accurate knowledge, confidence in procedures for seeking knowledge and the expectation through the use of verified knowledge were considered as the components of scientific attitude. The indicators of attitude towards science are hence;

- Willingness combined with open mindedness
- Critical reflection
- Removal of superstitions and false beliefs
- Spirit of healthy criticism.

Gakhar and Kaur (2004) identified the following components as attitude towards science: curiosity, open mindedness, faith in scientific method, cause and effect relationship, critical mindedness, seeks evidence, objectivity, suspended judgement and aversion to superstition.

Victor (1935) constructed an instrument based on six components. They are calculation, observation and report, intellectual honesty, open mindedness, the habit of suspended judgement and the habit of criticism.

Grewal (1990) constructed an Attitude Scale based on the following components: positive intellectual, negative intellectual, positive emotional and negative emotional attitudes.

Bhagwat (2006) constructed an Attitude Scale based on the following components: objectivity, verification, rational outlook, aversion and identification of cause and effect relationship.

The components covered in all these scales were studied and listed out. Different investigators had given different viewpoints in respect of inclusion of components in the scale. Out of them the investigator selected the following components for the ATS. They are curiosity, open mindedness, faith in scientific method, cause-effect relationship, critical mindedness, seeking evidence, objectivity, suspended judgement, elimination of belief in superstition, flexibility, critical approach to evaluation, facts with proofs, attitude to discover, respect for others views, biased/prejudiced notions, change of opinion after getting evidence etc. All these components were written in the format of most suitable, suitable and unsuitable and sent to thirteen experts in the field of science which included science academicians, professionals and science teachers teaching in secondary schools. The components selected by them as suitable for inclusion in the Attitude scale were considered and included in the scale. These components were then defined and items relating to these were framed.

3.4.3 Format/Techniques of the Construction of the Scale

After the selection of the components, the techniques of scale construction were thought of. Among the different techniques of constructing an attitude scale, the Likert method was considered to be the most suitable which was developed by Edwards (1957) on summated rating type.

While preparing the items for this scale, the criteria mentioned by Edwards (1957) had been followed. Precautions were taken to keep the reading level of the scale well within the reach of the normative pupils. The universe of content for the attitude scale constituted one hundred twenty (120) statements about science collected from various relevant sources dealing with the world of science. In the process of collecting, editing and selecting the statement, the informal criteria as suggested by Wang (1932), Thurstone and Chave (1929), Likert (1932), Bird (1940), Edwards (1957), Zilling (1928), Kar (1990) and Grewal (1990) were carefully observed.

With a view to knowing the nature of the statements, the edited items were submitted to a group of thirteen judges. These judges were specifically instructed to classify these 120 statements into two piles on the strength of the nature of the statement, positive and negative. Classifying any one of these items into neutral category was discouraged. They were then requested to read the statements with a view to point out, if any, flaws, omissions and commissions in the grammatical structure of the statements. Out of the 120 items, 87 were classified as positive while 33 as negative items. Suggestions offered by judges were incorporated in the statements to further refine and improve. The suggestions of experts and judges were taken note of and it was observed that out of 120 statements, only 100 items were selected to be incorporated in the scale having 75 positive items and 25 negative items.

3.4.4 Try-out of the Scale (ATS)

The scale (ATS) thus prepared consisting of 100 items were tried out over a representative sample of 200 students (100 boys and 100 Girls) following the precautions and principles of trying out a scale as follows. The selection of the try-out sample of 200 was made by following the simple random sampling procedure. Students from both Government and Non-Government schools of Bhubaneswar municipality area were listed and numbered as per the number written in the table of random numbers. From the table of random numbers, 200 sample were selected which consisted of 100 boys and 100 girls.

- It was observed that no other test/scale were administered over them that day in order to minimise the monotony and fatigue.
- Arrangements were properly made in respect of seating accommodation, light, ventilation noise free environment in order to minimise the extraneous effects.
- Enough spacing was maintained in respect of seating arrangement in order to minimise mutual discussion.
- Sufficient time was allowed to answer and give responses to each item of the scale as there was no fixed time limit but it was observed that all of them could respond within the stipulated time period of one hour and thirty minutes.
- All the respondents were thanked by the investigator for their ready responses and willingness to participate.

3.4.5 Scoring of the Response Sheets

The answered booklets containing the responses made by the students were then collected and scored according to the manual. The positive items were scored numerically 5, 4, 3, 2, 1 respectively for SA, A, UD, D, SD and negative items were scored in a reverse way of 1, 2, 3, 4, and 5 respectively for the same SA, A, UD, D and SD abbreviations. The attitude score of a student was considered as the sum total of scores on the hundred items scale by summating numerical scores on each of the items. Thus the scale had a minimum of 100 and maximum 500 on Attitude towards Science. After completion of scoring, the scale was subjected to item analysis.

3.4.6 Item Analysis of the Scale (ATS)

In order to analyse the statements in the Science Attitude Scale, all the attitude scores were arranged in

Table 3.1 Description of 75 Test Items with Score Points

Variation	*Test Items Serial Number*	*Total No. of Items*
Positive statements	2, 4, 5, 7, 8, 10, 11, 12, 13, 14, 16, 17, 19, 20, 22, 23, 25, 26, 28, 29, 31, 32, 34, 35, 36, 37, 38, 39, 40, 41, 42, 43, 44, 45, 46, 47, 51, 55, 56, 58, 62, 63, 64, 65, 66, 67, 68, 70, 71, 72, 73, 74, 75,	53
Negative statements	1, 3, 6, 9, 15, 18, 21, 24, 27, 30, 33, 48, 49, 50, 52, 53, 54, 57, 59, 60, 61, 69	22
	Total	75

Table 3.2 Sub-components of the Attitude towards Science Scale

Categories / sub Components		*Test Items Number*
1.	Elimination of belief in superstitions	17, 48*, 51, 61*
2.	Curiosity to know	11, 12, 13, 28, 29, 34, 37, 56, 62, 63, 66, 67, 68, 71, 72, 74
3.	Open mindedness	18*, 19, 30*, 35, 41, 47, 49*, 53*, 54, 55, 64, 69*, 70, 73
4.	Facts with proofs	4,5, 6*, 7, 8, 10, 14, 16, 23, 25, 26, 36, 38, 39, 40, 42, 43, 44
5.	Critical evaluation	1*, 2, 20, 31, 32, 33*, 60*, 65, 75
6.	Change of opinion after getting evidence	3*, 9*, 15*, 21*, 24*, 27*, 50*, 52*, 59*
7.	Attitude to discover	22, 45, 46
8.	Respect for other views	57* , 58

**indicates negative items.*

order of size of the scale score. The procedure for item analysis was adopted as per the formula suggested by Garett, 1961 for discriminating power and Guilford, 1965 for phi-coefficients selection of items for the final scale was done by taking into consideration high values of discriminating power and phi-coefficients of the items as indices of item validity. The values of phi-coefficients of the items which have been retained were found to be significant at 0.01 level of significance. For determining the discriminating power the difference between the weighted means in the high and low scoring groups which ranged from 2.16 to 3.40 and phi-coefficients from 0.50 to 0.87 were considered. Thus, the scale Attitude towards Science consisted of 75 items having 53 positive and 22 negative items. Thus, the scale Attitude towards Science developed by Mishra (2008) consisted of 53 positive items and 22 negative items.

3.4.7 Study of Normality on the Scores of Attitude towards Science

In order to study the normality in distribution of scores on attitude towards science, the descriptive measures of Mean, Median, Mode, Quartile deviation and Percentile of scores on attitude towards science scale were calculated and presented in Table 3.3.

The distribution of scores on the ATS scale ranges from 246 to 354, the mean of the scores has been calculated to be 304.85 and the median is 307.3 above and below the mean lie 54.5 and 45.5 per cent of cases. The class interval 305-314 contains the highest percentage (25 per cent) which is treated as the modal class interval and frequencies decrease on both sides of the modal class interval. But the decrease is abrupt towards the higher end compared to the lower end. The standard deviation of the distribution being 23.92, sixty seven per cent of the cases fall within the mean ± 1ä limits as against 68.26 per cent of scores in case of

Table 3.3 Descriptive Measures on Attitude towards Science Scores of the Total Sample

Variation		*N*	*Mean*	*Median*	*Mode*	*SD*	P_{90}	P_{10}	Q_3	Q_1	*Q*
Gen-der	Boys	100	303.23	306.2	312.14	23.32	328	272.5	314	289	312.14
	Girls	100	302.3	305.12	310.76	22.89	329	265.5	315.5	283.5	310.76
Total		200	304.85	307.3	312.2	23.92	330	268.5	314	286	312.2

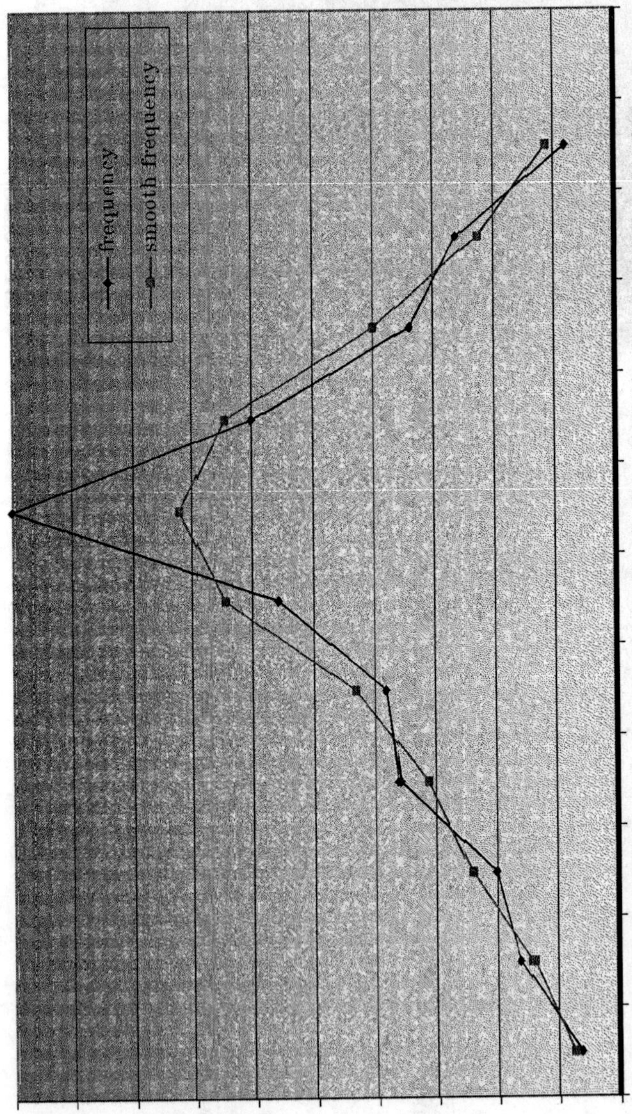

Fig. 3.1: Frequency Polygon on ATS Scores with Smoothed Frequency Curve Super Imposed.

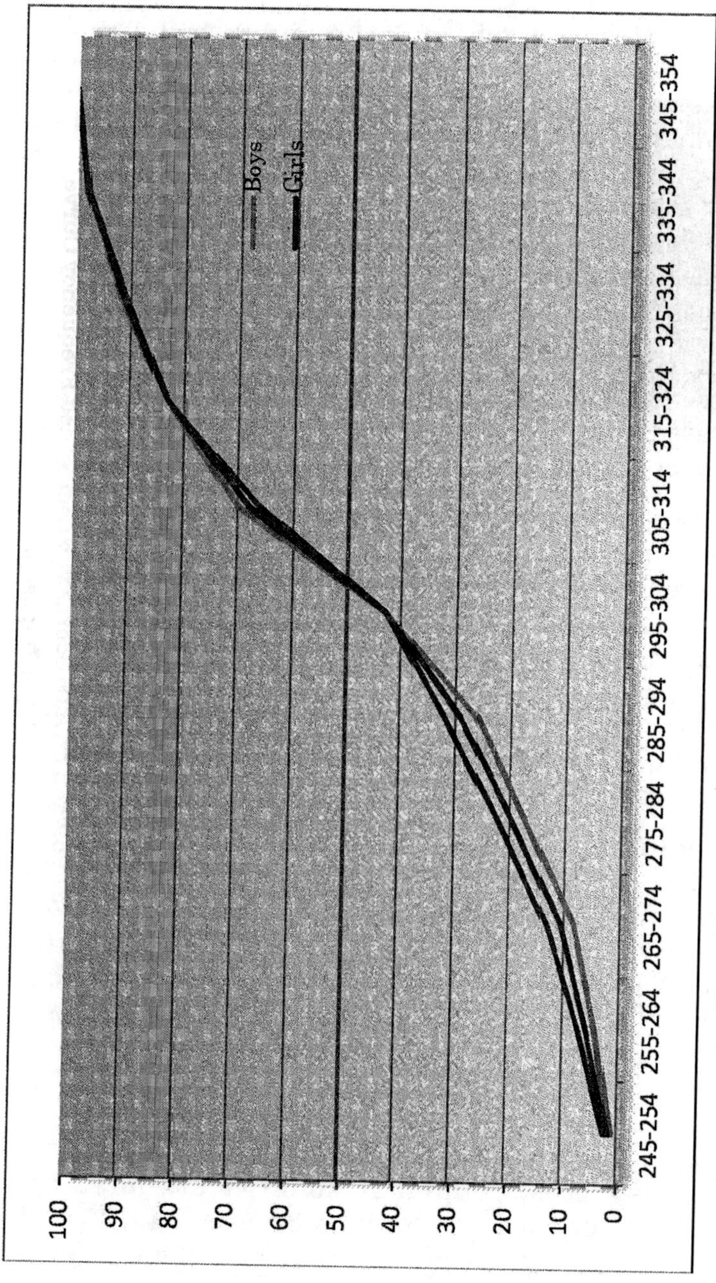

Fig. 3.2: Ogive on the Scores on the Attitude towards Science.

normal distribution 96 per cent of scores within ± 2 ä limits as against 95.44 per cent of cases. The Skewness and Kurtosis of the curve give ample evidence in respect of the nature of the curve. The Skewness was found to be negatively skewed (-.261) indicating higher range of scores at the right side of the curve. Such a tendency in the high score range may be attributed to the nature of response applicable to the rating scales in behavioural science.

The Kurtosis of the curve was found to be 0.11 which is less than the normal value of 0.263. This tendency indicated that the normal curve drawn on attitude scores for the total sample was leptokurtic in nature.

3.4.8 Evaluation of the Scale (ATS)

In order to judge the scale for its efficiency, consistency and adequacy as a measuring instrument, it was considered necessary to evaluate the scale by estimating its reliability, validity and determining its norms for wider implementation or use. The details of the procedure for giving evidence in support of validity and reliability have been described in the following paragraphs.

3.4.9 Reliability of the ATS Scale

The reliability of the ATS scale now consisting of 75 items was measured through test-retest method over the representative sample of 200 who had not taken the test earlier, but represented the same population from which the sample was drawn. The same scale was again administered over the same sample after a month and the co-efficient of correlation between the two sets of scores obtained through Pearson Product Moment Method was found to be 0.78. Sood (1975), Grewal (1990) found test-retest reliability co-efficients for their attitude scales (Attitude towards Science) as 0.76 and 0.77 respectively. However, Bhagwat (2006) had a test-retest reliability co-efficient or the Scientific Attitude Scale as 0.94, Gakhar and Kaur (2004) found a reliability co-efficient of 0.70. In view of the above observations, the reliability co-efficient of the present Attitude towards Science Scale was considered satisfactory. The dependability of the scale ATS was studied as an estimate of the reliability co-efficient in terms of standard error of measurement as suggested by Guilford (1965), Ferguson (1986) and Garett (1961). The standard error of measurement of the scale was estimated to be 11.01 which was small and when it is small, it is presumed that a degree of confidence in the true score is not far away is built (Guilford and Frutcher, 1978). Based upon the above observations, the Attitude towards Science Scale developed by the investigator with a reliability co-efficient of 0.78 and a standard error of measurement of 11.01 was considered as a reliable instrument for measuring the secondary school students' attitude towards science.

3.4.10 Validity of the Scale (ATS)

The validity evidence in its content and internal validity have been established through the inclusion of items of the scale, quite representative of wide areas on attitude towards science, experts views on judgement of items to be included in the scale component wise. The internal validity evidence has been supported through 't'-values (Edwards, 1957). Every statement included in the final scale has 't'- value of 1.98 and above.

The criterion related evidence to validity has been established by calculating the concurrent evidence to validity through correlating the scores with the scores obtained by the respondents on Grewal's (1990) Science Attitude Scale and the validity index obtained was 0.464 which was highly significant.

Kar (1990) found a concurrent validity index of 0.60. Gakhar and Kaur (2004) found out content validity on his scientific Attitude Scale. Basing upon these observations, the validity co-efficient on this scale, evidences to content and internal validity the scale was considered valid and the measuring instrument was considered as a good tool to assess the attitude of students towards science.

3.4.11 Fixation of Norms

In order to facilitate interpretation of the scores of the tools developed, table of norms have been provided for the Attitude scale. The norms have been presented in this respect in terms of percentiles, standard scores and stanines.

3.4.12 Percentile Norms

In presenting the percentile norms developed by the investigator, care has been taken to indicate the relative position of a score in relation to all other scores in the distribution. This permits the investigator to express how well an individual has performed as compared to all other individuals in the sample who have been measured on the same variable. A percentile rank indicates the percentage of scores that fall below a given score. Therefore, such a measure is frequently used in reporting test results. The percentile scores have been calculated from the distribution of scores on ATS. The percentile norms of the distribution are given as here under:

Table 3.4. Percentile Norms on ATS Scale

Percentile Norms	*Boys*	*Girls*	*Total*
P_{90}	328	329	330.00
P_{75}	314	315.5	314.00
P_{50}	312.14	310.76	312.20
P_{25}	289	283.5	286.00
P_{10}	272.5	265.5	268.50

3.4.13 Standard Scores

In order to express how far a given raw score is from the mean in terms of standard deviation units, the standard scores have been calculated and stanine points have been determined. The stanines have been considered to calculate different categories of students having attitude towards science. The result has been presented in Table 3.5.

Table 3.5: Stanine Norms alongwith Score Range on the ATS and Categories in the Sample

Stanine Grades	*In Terms of SD Scores*	*Score Range*
9	+ 1.75 and above	350 and above
8	+ 1.25 to 1.75	338-350
7	+0.75 to 1.25	326-338
6	+0.25 to 0.75	314-326
5	± 0.25	302-314
4	-0.25 to -0.75	290-302
3	-0.75 to -1.25	278-290
2	-1.25 to -1.75	266-278
1	-1.75 and below	Below 266

3.4.14 Categorisation of the Sample

Basing upon the norms the scores obtained by the students were divided into five categories in order of level of attitude scores on ATS. They were superior, above average, average, below average and poor. For this the categorisation was made on the basis of Normal curve split into five equal parts. It was revealed that there were 10, 51, 80, 48 and 11 students in order of very high level attitude, high level, average level, poor level and very poor level of attitude respectively.

4

Analysis of Attitude Towards Science

This chapter is devoted to organisation and collection of data according to the objectives and hypotheses formulated and intended to present an analysis of the results that had been obtained through the application of the method and procedure mentioned earlier. The results are presented in tables followed by discussion. The findings are corroborated with earlier researches for confirmation of the result by sighting research studies predicting the same or different results by including these variables. The results are organised under differential analysis and study of relationship on the variables and between the variables.

4.1 Study of Normality on the Scores of Attitude Towards Science (ATS)

The scores of Attitude towards Science were tabulated and scores of the sample were given as follows according to the scores of sub-samples that were boys and girls. The Attitude towards Science scores were compiled and the highest and the lowest scores were found. The scores ranged from 206-343 in case of girls, 198-328 in case of boys and 198-343 in case of total. In order to study the normality in distribution of scores

Table 4.1: Descriptive Measures on Attitude towards Science Scores of the Total Sample

Variation		*N*	*Mean*	*Md*	*Mode*	*SD*	P_{90}	P_{10}	Q_3	Q_1	*Q*
Gen-der	Boys	189	264.74	269	280	21.83	291	233	280	249	15.5
	Girls	211	270.16	271	257	2048	294.8	247	284	257	13.5
Total		400	267.87	269	271.44	21.30	293.53	238.08	281.99	253.81	14.0

Note: {Recheck this Table}

on Attitude towards Science, the descriptive measures of Mean, Median, Mode, Standard Deviation, Quartile Deviation and Percentile of Scores on Attitude towards Science scale were calculated and presented in Table 4.1.

From the Table 4.1 it was inferred that the sample mean, medians and mode are found to be 267.87, 269.06 and 271.44 respectively. The semi-interquartile range of the distribution of scores being 14.09, the sum of the median and semi-quartile range was found to be 283.15 and the difference between the two was 254.97. The third and first quartile of the distribution were 281.99 and 253.81 respectively.

If the sum and the difference between the median and the semi-interquartile range became the same with the third and the first quartile respectively, then they gave the evidence towards normality in distribution of scores on Attitude towards Science. As in the above given case, it was approximately the same, hence it was inferred that the distribution was normal distribution. The distribution of Attitude towards Science scores had been studied by plotting the scores as per the normal distribution. The result indicated that the mean, median and mode of the distribution did not coincide and the distribution was both influenced by Skewness and Kurtosis. The Skewness of the normal probability curve was -0.16 as against 0 in case of normal value and kurtosis was found to be 0.254 as against the normal value of 0.263. This indicated that the distribution of scores from normality stand point was negatively skewed and leptokurtic but the magnitude of difference was very small. Considering the result investigation was mentioned to conclude that the result obtained due to the investigation was almost normal bearing aside the slight abnormality due to sampling error. This could be better understood with the help of the following figures. The frequencies and smoothed frequencies had been

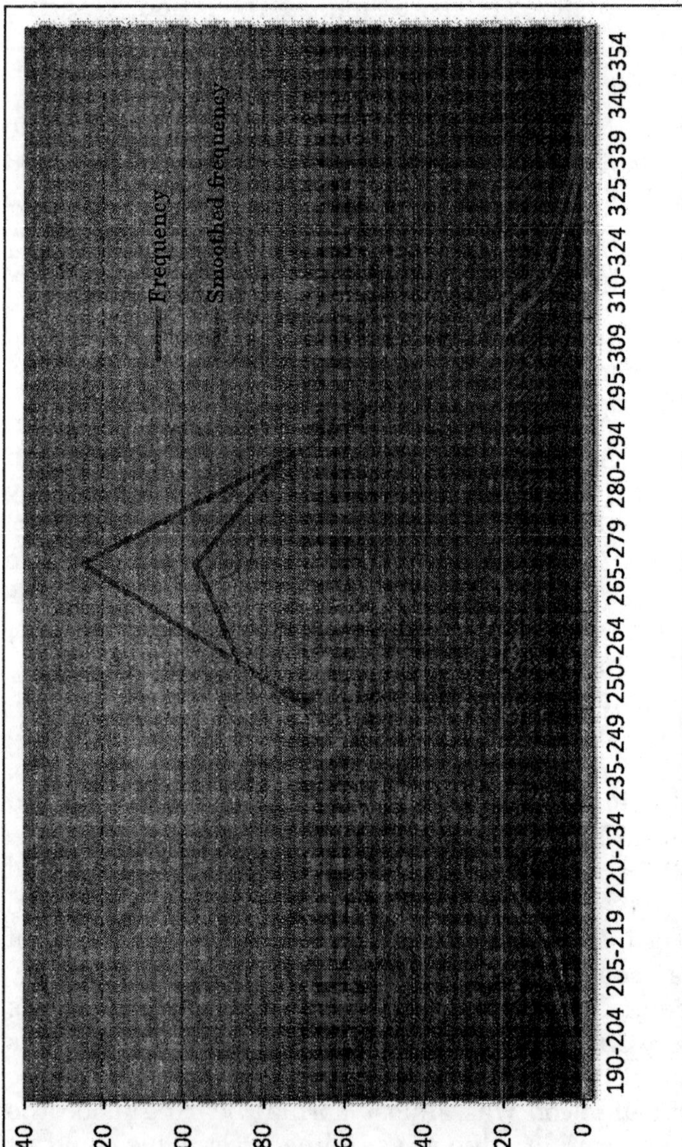

Fig. 4.1: Normal Probability Curve with Smoothed Frequency Super-imposed of Total Sample on Attitude Towards Science Scores.

plotted into a frequency polygon curve with the smoothed frequency polygon super-imposed on it.

4.2 Study of Normality on the Scores of Intelligence Test

The scores of Intelligence test were tabulated and scores of the samples were given as follows according to the scores of sub-samples that were boys and girls. The Intelligence scores were compiled and the highest and the lowest scores were found. The scores ranged from 19-79 in case of girls, 14-79 in case of boys and 14-79 in case of total. In order to study the normality in distribution of scores on Intelligence test, the descriptive measures of Mean, Median, Mode, Standard Deviation, Quartile Deviation and percentile of scores on Intelligence test were calculated and presented in Table 4.2.

From the Table 4.2 it was inferred that the sample mean, median and mode were found to be 45.125, 44.68 and 43.79 respectively. The semi-inter-quartile range of the distribution of scores being 8.675, the sum of the median and semi-quartile range was found to be 53.355 and the difference between the two was 36.005. The third and first quartiles of the distribution were 53.59 and 36.24 respectively.

If the sum and the difference between the median and the semi-inter-quartile range became the same with the third and the first quartile respectively, then they gave the evidence towards normality in distribution of scores on Intelligence scale. As in the above given case, it was approximately the same, hence it was inferred that the distribution was normal distribution. The distribution of Intelligence scores had been studied by plotting the scores as per the normal distribution. The result indicated that the mean, median and mode of the distribution were both influenced by skewness and

Table 4.2: Descriptive Measures on Intelligence Scores of the Total Sample

Variation		*N*	*Mean*	*Md.*	*Mode*	*SD*	P_{90}	P_{10}	Q_3	Q_1	*Q*
Gender	Boys	189	48.04	47.77	47.23	22.38	66.62	30.2	57.15	40.03	8.56
	Girls	211	42.50	42.19	41.57	21.24	53.30	28.5	49.13 8	34.29	7.42
Total		400	45.125	44.68	43.79	15.41	62.73	29.5	53.59	36.24	8.67

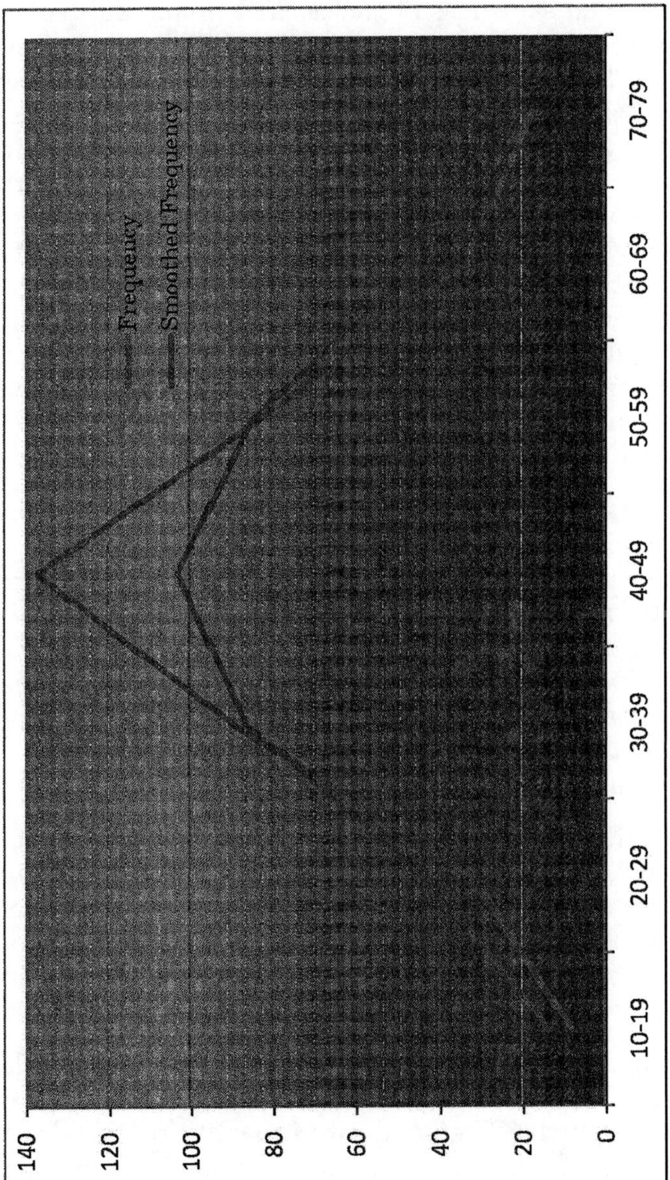

Fig. 4.2 : Normal Probability Curve with Smoothed Frequency Superimposed of Total Sample on Intelligence Scores.

kurtosis. The skewness of the normal probability curve was 0.08 as against 0 in case of normal value and kurtosis was found to be 0.260 as against the normal value of 0.263. This indicated that the distribution of scores from normality stand point was positively skewed and leptokurtic but the magnitude of difference was very small. Considering the result investigation was mentioned to conclude that the result obtained due to the investigation was almost normal leaving aside the slight abnormality due to sampling error. This could be better understood with the help of the following figures. The frequencies and smoothed frequencies had been plotted into a frequency polygon curve with the smoothed frequency polygon super-imposed on it.

4.3 Study of Normality on the Scores of Socio-economic Status Scale

The scores of socio-economic status scale were tabulated and scores of the sample were given as follows according to the scores of sub samples that were boys and girls. The socio-economic status scores were compiled and the highest and the lowest scores were found. The scores ranged from 6 to 29 in case of girls, 7 to 29 in case of boys and 6 to 29 in case of total.

In order to study the normality in distribution of scores on socio-economic status scale, the descriptive measures of Mean, Median, Mode, Standard Deviation, Quartile Deviation and Percentile of scores on socio-economic status scale were calculated and presented in Table 4.3.

From the Table 4.3 it was inferred that the sample mean, median and mode are found to be 23.1, 23.0 and 27.0 respectively. The semi-inter-quartile range of the distribution of scores being 2.89, the sum of the median and semi-quartile range was found to be 25.89 and the difference between the two was 20.11. The third and

Table 4.3: Descriptive Measures on Socio-economic Status Scores of the Total Sample

Variation		*N*	*Mean*	*Md.*	*Mode*	*SD*	P_{90}	P_{10}	Q_3	Q_1	*Q*
Gender	Boys	189	22.7	23.0	27.0	3.6	47.62	15.3	21.10	15.19	2.95
	Girls	211	23.6	23.0	27.0	3.4	48.45	14.35	20.44	14.79	2.82
Total		400	23.1	23.0	27.0	3.6	23.45	12.25	20.75	14.96	2.89

first quartiles of the distribution were 20.75 and 14.96 respectively.

If the sum and the difference between the median and the semi-inter-quartile range became the same with the third and the first quartile respectively, then they gave the evidence towards normality in distribution of scores on socio-economic status scale. As in the above given case, it was approximately the same, hence it was inferred that the distribution was normal distribution. The distribution of socio-economic status scores had been studied by plotting the scores as per the normal distribution. The result indicated that the mean, median and mode of the distribution did not coincide and the distribution was both influenced by skewness and kurtosis. The skewness of the normal probability curve was 0.08 as against 0 in case of normal value and kurtosis was found to be 0.258 as against the normal value of 0.263. This indicated that the distribution of scores from normality stand point was positively skewed and leptokurtic but the magnitude of difference was very small. Considering the result investigation was mentioned to conclude that the result obtained due to the investigation was almost normal leaving aside the slight abnormality due to sampling error.

This could be better understood with the help of the following Figure 4.3. The frequencies and smoothed frequencies had been plotted into a frequency polygon curve with the smoothed frequency polygon superimposed on it.

4.3.1 Classification of Subjects into Socio-economic Status Groups

In order to analyse the data further the entire sample were classified with reference to mean and standard deviation of the distribution, into two categories such as higher socio-economic status group and lower

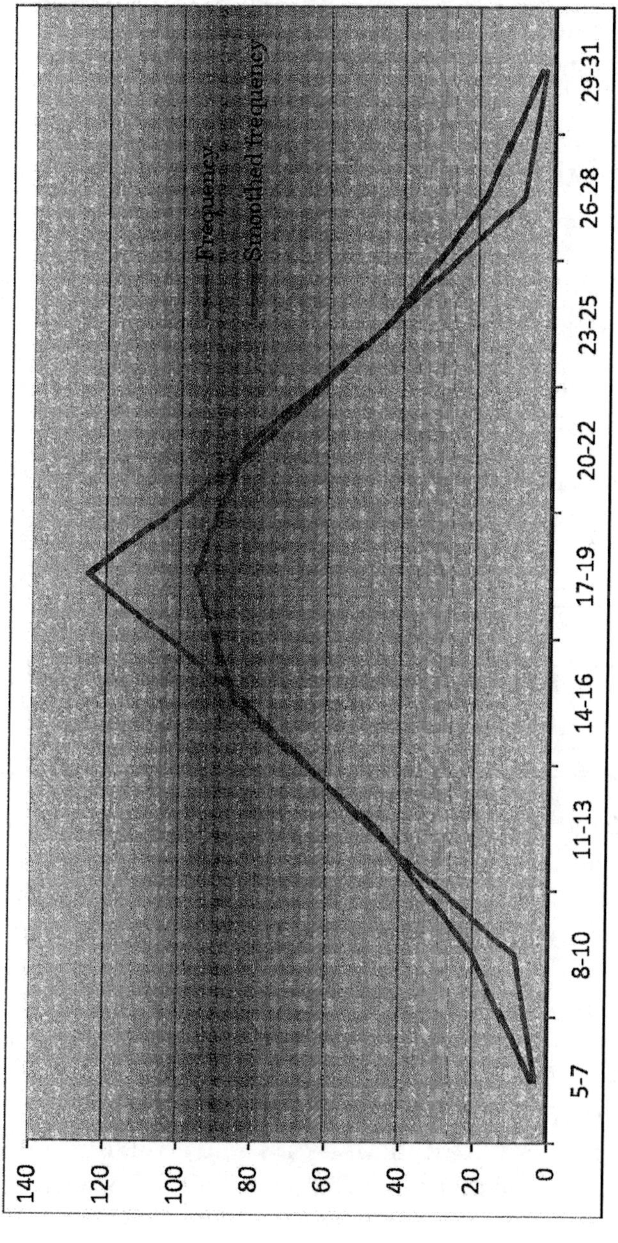

Fig. 4.3 : Normal Probability Curve with Smoothed Frequency Superimposed of Total Sample on Socio-economic Status Scores.

socio-economic status group. It was observed that out of 400 respondents, 191 students belonged to the high socio-economic status group whereas 209 students fell into the low socio-economic status group. The cut off score between the high and low socio-economic status groups was the median students having a score on socio-economic status above the median were considered under the high socio-economic status group whereas students having the score points below the median points were considered the low socio-economic status category. The mean and standard deviation of high and low socio-economic status group were calculated and presented in Table 4.3.1.

Table 4.3.1: Mean and Standard Deviation of the High Socio-economic Status and Low Socio-economic Status Groups

Variation	*Sub sample*	*N*	*M*	*SD*
Socio-economic Status	High SES	191	272.75	15.26
	Low SES	209	266.45	12.23

4.4 Study of School Environmental Condition

The school environmental condition of the responding school was studied by administrating the Information Schedule on School Environmental Condition developed by Parida (1994). Scoring of Information Schedule on School Environmental Condition was done as per the scoring scheme described under method of study. However, the factors which were of demographic nature were compiled in terms of percentage. A detailed list of such environmental condition had been presented in accordance with the items of the scale.

As the schools were taken from Cuttack and Bhubaneswar city, there were deviations in respect of staff strength, teachers' academic and professional qualifications. The total scores on teacher input, material input and process inputs were calculated and a school having 450 or above score points were earmarked as schools having adequate facilities and below that the schools were demarcated as schools having inadequate facilities. Among eighteen schools, twelve schools had adequate facilities and only six schools had inadequate facilities.

A detailed study in the three inputs, teacher, material and process inputs when was made it was observed that in all the sections the schools having adequate facilities were visibly better than the schools of inadequate facilities in respect of material and process inputs only. Therefore, the investigator had attempted to compare the schools having adequate facilities with the schools having inadequate facilities in respect of teacher, material and process inputs.

4.5 Categorisation of the Sample on Attitude Towards Science

After presenting the measures of central tendency and variation it was thought obligatory to categorise the sample according to differential degree of attitude

Table 4.5: Percentage of Sample on Differential Level of Attitude towards Science

Category	*Percentage*
High	3
Above Average	15
Average	62
Below Average	17
Low	3
Total	100

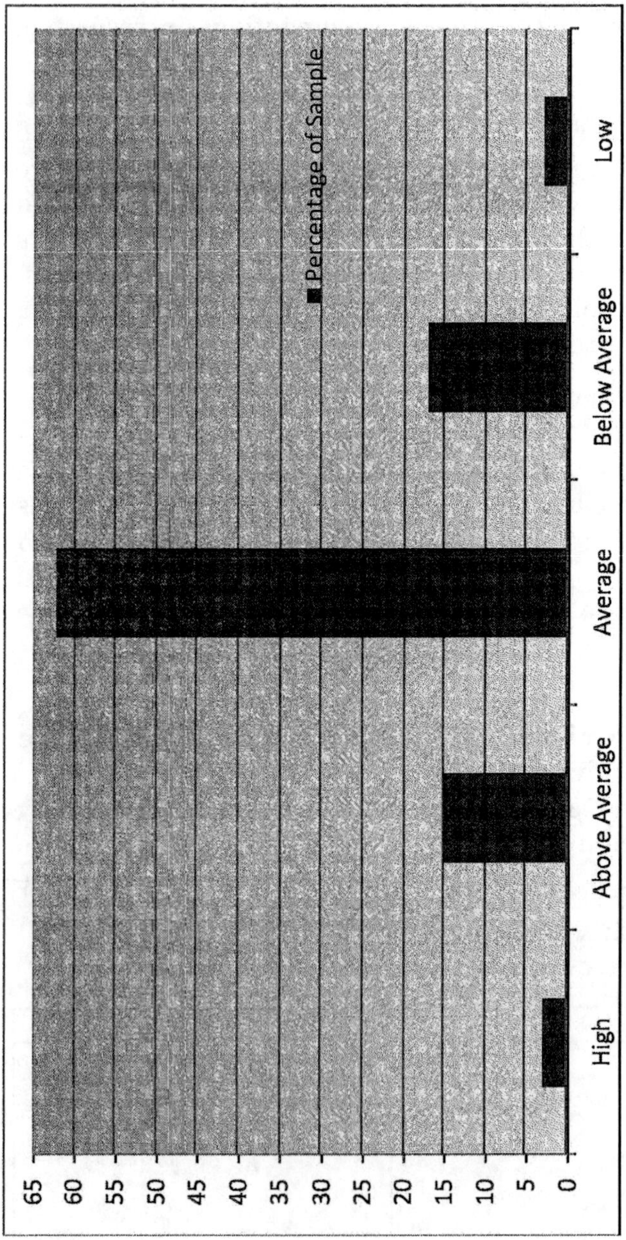

Fig. 4.5: Categorisation of the Samples on Attitude Towards Science.

towards science in students. For this the cut off marks for high, above average, average, below average and low was decided. The sample was presented in the Table 4.5 below.

On perusal of the above table, it was evident that out of the entire sample of 400 students, 248 students had average positive attitude, 12 students possessed high positive attitude, 60 students had above average positive attitude, 68 students had below average positive attitude and only 12 students had low positive attitude towards science. The percentage of the sample in different categories had been presented graphically in terms of a histogram in Figure below.

4.6 Categorisation of the Sample According to Sub-samples

The sample had been splitted into nine categories. They were:

- Boys *Vs.* Girls
- High Socio-Economic Status *Vs.* Low Socio-Economic Status
- High Intelligence *Vs.* Low Intelligence
- Government school students Vs Non-government school students
- Boys school *Vs.* Girls school
- Boys school *Vs.* Co-education school
- Girls school *Vs.* Co-education school
- Adequate school environment *Vs.* Inadequate school environment
- High achieving schools *Vs.* Low achieving schools

Table 4.6. Descriptive Measures on Attitude towards Science Scores

Variables		*N*	*Mean*	*Md.*	*Mode*	*SD*	P_{90}	Q_3	Q_2	Q_1	P_{10}
Gender	Boys	189	264.74	269	280	21.834	291	280	269	249	23
	Girls	211	270.16	271	257	20.487	294.8	284	271	257	247
SES	High	191	272.75	270.5	270	15.26	294	284	270.5	255	239
	Low	209	266.45	269	276	12.23	291	280	269	253	240
Int.	High	73	270.99	270	284	14.1	292	281.75	270	254.25	237.2
	Low	55	263.39	269.5	257	12.2	293.9	280	269.5	254	240.1
Env.	Adeq.	220	265.90	269	276	22.334	292	280	269	250.25	234
	Inadeq.	180	269.68	270.5	259	19.779	294	281	270.5	250.25	247.1
School Type	Boys	120	266.99	270	280	21.693	291.9	280	270	253	237
	Girls	140	269.71	270.5	257	19.971	294	281.75	270.5	257	246.1
	Co-ed.	140	266.01	269.5	245	22.154	291.9	281	269.5	250.50	236.2
Mngt.	Govt.	180	265.27	268	257	22.163	292.9	280	268	250	237
	Non-govt.	220	269.50	271	259	20.382	292.9	283	271	257	245

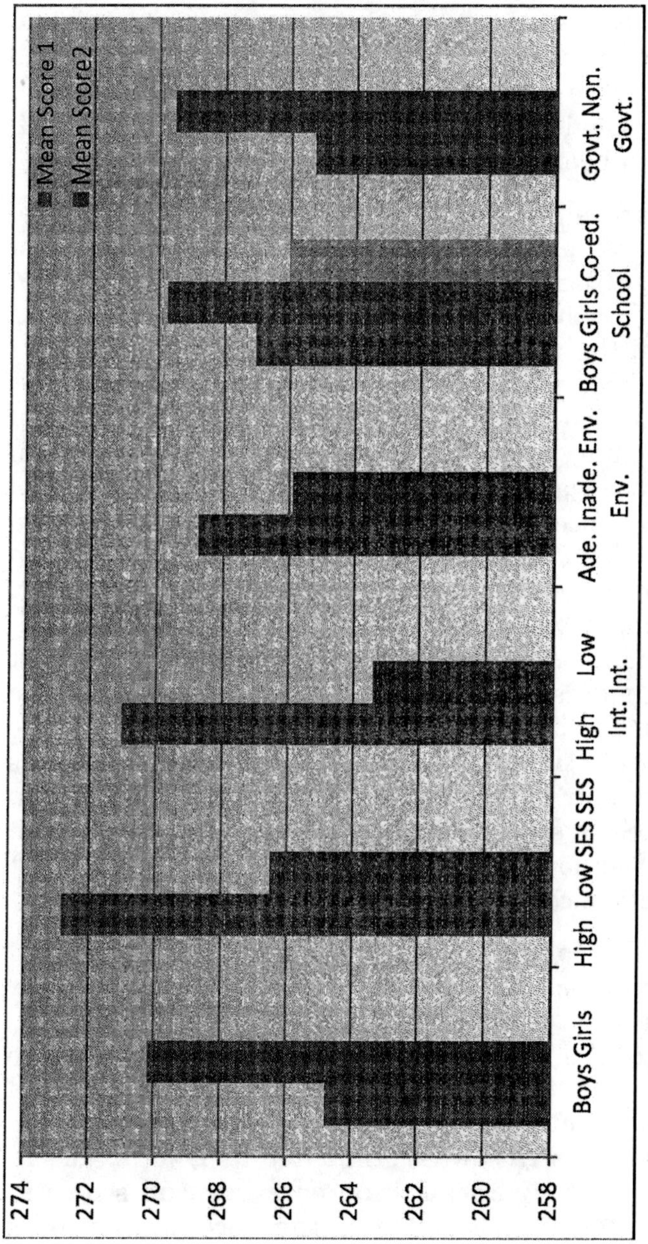

Fig. 4.6: Mean Scores on Attitude towards Science According to Sub-samples.

4.6.1 Descriptive Measures on Attitude Towards Science Scores

After categorisation of the samples according to sub samples, Mean, Median, Mode, Standard Deviation, Quartile Deviation and Percentiles were calculated. These had been presented in the Table 4.7.

On perusal of the Table 4.7 it was observed that the mean scores on attitude towards science of boys and girls differ from the total mean, girls having more mean scored than boys. In case of socio-economic status variation, the mean score of high socio-economic status on attitude towards science scale was slightly higher than mean score of low socio-economic status. In case of Intelligence variation, the mean score of high Intelligence was slightly higher than the mean score of low intelligence. In case of school environment, the mean score of adequate school environment was higher than the inadequate school environment. In case of type of management variation, the ATTS mean score of non-Government students was higher than the Government school students. In case of type of school variation, the ATTS mean score of Girls school was higher than the Boys school. The ATTS mean score of Boys school was almost similar to co-education school. The ATTS mean score of Girls school was higher than the co-education school. Therefore, differential analysis was made to test the significance of the difference.

4.7 Analysis of Attitude Towards Science of Secondary School Students in Relation to Gender Variation

One of the objectives of the study was to estimate the Attitude towards Science of secondary school students in relation to gender variation. For this the null hypothesis HO_1 was formulated as follows, "There does not exist significant difference in mean scores in Attitude towards Science of the secondary school

Table 4.7: Test of Significance of Difference on Attitude towards Science Scores due to Gender Variation

Variation	*Sub-sample*	*N*	*M*	*SD*	*SED*	*'t'*	*Remark*
Gender	Boys	189	264.74	21.834			
	Girls	211	270.16	20.487	2.117	2.55	S

P values of t at 0.05 = 1.96, 0.01 = 2.58 for df 398.

students in relation to gender variation." In order to test the gender differences in Attitude towards Science the 't' ratio had been calculated and presented below:

It was quite evident from the Table 4.7 that the obtained value of 't' ratio was 2.55 which was greater than the table value 1.96 at 0.05 level and 2.58 at 0.01 level of significance. Hence the 't' ratio (2.55) in case of gender variation was significant at 0.05 level. So the null hypothesis HO_1 that "there is no significant difference in mean scores on Attitude towards Science Scale of the secondary school students in relation to gender variation" could be rejected and concluded that there was difference between boys and girls in their Attitude towards Science.

The result was in conformity with earlier studies conducted by Ghosh (1990), Mandila (1990), Darchingpuii (1990), Alexander (1990), Nelliapa (1992) and Lightbody and Durnbell (1996) who had shown gender as an intervening variable for Attitude towards Science. Based upon the result cited above, the investigator was inclined to conclude the result to be appropriate.

4.8 Analysis of Attitude Towards Science of Secondary School Students in relation to Differential Levels of Socio-economic Status

The objective of the study was to estimate the Attitude towards Science of secondary school students in relation to socio-economic status variation. For this the null hypothesis HO_2 was formulated as follows, "There does not exist significant difference in mean scores on Attitude towards Science of secondary school students in relation to differential levels of socio-economic status". For the appropriateness of the study, 't' ratio was calculated as shown in the Table 4.8.

Table 4.8: Test of Significance of Difference on Attitude towards Science Scores due to Differential Levels of Socio-economic Status

Variation	*Sub-sample*	*N*	*M*	*SD*	*SED*	*'t'*	*Remark*
SES	High SES	191	272.75	15.26	5.22	1.20	NS
	Low SES	209	266.45	12.23			

P value of t at 0.05= 1.96, 0.01 = 2.58 for df 298.

On the above given data it was quite evident that the obtained value of 't' ratio was 1.20 and less than the table value which is 1.96 at 0.05 level of significance and 2.58 at 0.01 level of significance. Hence the 't' ratio could not be significant. So the null hypothesis HO_2 that "there is no significant difference in mean scores on Attitude towards Science of secondary school students in relation to differential levels of Socio Economic Status" could not be rejected and it was concluded that there was no difference between students of high Socio-economic Status and low Socio-economic Status on their Attitude towards Science. The result was in conformity with earlier studies conducted by Ghosh (1990), Darchingpuii (1990) and Alexander (1990) who had shown that Socio economic Status did not play any role on the Attitude towards Science of the students. Based upon the result cited above, the investigator concluded the result to be appropriate.

4.9 Analysis of Attitude Towards Science of Secondary School Students in Relation to Differential Levels of Intelligence

The objective of the study was to determine the difference in Attitude towards Science of secondary school students due to the personal variables of Intelligence. For this the null hypothesis HO_3 was formulated as follows, "There exists no significant difference in mean scores on Attitude towards Science of secondary school students in relation to differential levels of Intelligence. The scores on attitude towards science were also categorised under group of high intelligence and low intelligence. For this the cut off marks was above +2 ä distance from the mean for the high group and below -2ä distance from the means as the low group. As such in both the groups of high and low it was observed that there were 73 and 55 students respectively. In order to find out the significance of

Table 4.9: Test of Significance of Difference on Attitude towards Science Scores due to Differential Levels of Intelligence

Variation	*Sub-sample*	*N*	*M*	*SD*	*SED*	*'t'*	*Remark*
Intelligence	High Intelligence	73	270.99	14.1	2.32	3.27	S
	Low Intelligence	55	263.39	12.2			

P values of t at 0.05 = 1.96, 0.01 = 2.58.

difference in mean attitude towards science score of differential levels of intelligence group like high and low, the 't' ratio was calculated and result was presented in Table 4.9.

From the Table 4.9, it was observed that the obtained value of 't' ratio that was 3.27, was greater than the table value which was 1.96 at 0.05 level of significance and 2.58 at 0.01 level of significance. Hence the 't' ratio was significant. So the null hypothesis HO_3 that 'there is no significant difference in mean scores on Attitude towards Science of secondary school students in relation to differential levels of Intelligence" was rejected and concluded that there was significant difference between students of high intelligence and low intelligence on their Attitude Towards Science. The result was in conformity with earlier studies conducted by Darchingpuii (1990), Alexander (1990), Raghavan (1991) and Ahamad, Raheem and Hasan (2003) who had shown that Intelligence is the intervening variable for Attitude towards Science. Based upon the result cited above, the investigator concluded that the result might be considered appropriate.

4.10 Analysis of Attitude Towards Science of Secondary School Students in Relation to Type of Management

One of the objectives of the study was to determine the difference in attitude towards science of secondary school students in relation to type of management. For this the null hypothesis HO_4 was formulated as follows, "there exists no significant difference in Attitude towards Science of secondary school students in relation to the institutional variables (Type of Management)." For the verification of null hypothesis, the 't' ratio was calculated and presented in Table 4.10.

Table 4.10: Test of Significance of Difference on Attitude towards Science Scores due to Type of Management

Variation	*Sub-sample*	*N*	*M*	*SD*	*SED*	*'t'*	*Remark*
Type of Management	Govt. School	180	265.27	22.163			
	Non-govt. School	220	269.50	20.382	2.131	1.98	S

P values of t at 0.05 = 1.96, 0.01 = 2.58.

It was quite evident from the Table 4.10 that the obtained value of 't' ratio being 1.98 greater than the tabular value 1.96 at 0.05 level of significance, was significant. Therefore significant difference between the students of Government Schools and Non-Government Schools in their attitude towards science was confirmed. The result was in conformity with earlier studies conducted by Simpson and Oliver (1990), Myers and Fonts (1992), Darchingpuii (1990), Nelliapa (1992) and Adesoji (2008) who had shown that school management played a significant role in differentiating Attitude towards Science in students. Based upon the result cited above, the investigator desired to conclude that the result might be considered appropriate.

4.11. Analysis of Attitude Towards Science of Secondary School Students in Relation to Type of School

Attitude towards Science of secondary school students in relation to type of school was also tested for significance between the contrasts relating to type of school variation through 't' ratio. The result presented below revealed that the 't' ratio was non-significant in each case.

So the null hypothesis HO_4 that 'there exists no significant difference in Attitude towards Science of secondary school students in relation to the institutional variables (type of school)' could not be rejected. The study was in conformity with earlier studies conducted by Simpson and Oliver (1990) and Darchingpuii (1990) who had shown that type of schools did not play any role in the Attitude towards Science of the students. Based upon the result cited above, the investigator desired to conclude that the result might be considered appropriate.

Table 4.11: Test of Significance of Difference on Attitude towards Science Scores due to Type of School

Variation	*Sub-sample*	*N*	*M*	*SD*	*SED*	*'t'*	*Remark*
Type of School	Boys School	120	266.99	21.693	2.585	1.050	NS
	Girls School	140	269.71	19.971			
	Co-education School	140	266.01	22.154	2.730	0.361	NS
	Boys School	120	266.99	21.693			
	Girls School	140	269.71	19.971	2.521	1.468	NS
	Co-education School	140	266.01	22.154			

P values of t at 0.05 = 1.96, 0.01 = 2.58.

Table 4.12: Test of Significance of Difference on Attitude towards Science Scores due to School Environment

Variation	*Sub sample*	*N*	*M*	*SD*	*SED*	*'t'*	*Remark*
School Environment	Adequate	220	269.68	19.779	2.112	1.99	S
	Inadequate	180	265.90	22.334			

P values of t at 0.05 = 1.96, 0.01 = 2.58.

4.12 Analysis of Attitude Towards Science of Secondary School Students in Relation to School Environment

The objective of the study was to determine the difference in Attitude towards Science of secondary school students in relation to school environment. For this the null hypothesis HO_4 "there exists no significant difference in Attitude towards Science of secondary school students in relation to the institutional variables of school environment was formulated. For the verification of null hypothesis, the 't' ratio was calculated and presented in Table 4.12. As stated earlier, the school environment was studied in the context of facilities available for teaching of science and atmosphere prevailed in the institution for this. Therefore the school environment was considered in terms of adequate and inadequate environments.

From the Table 4.12, it was observed that the 't' ratio was 1.99 which indicated that the difference in attitude towards science was observed between the students of adequate and inadequate school environment. This gave the idea that the schools having facilities for teaching of science with all necessary materials developed proper attitude in students towards science. The result was in conformity with earlier studies conducted by Simpson and Oliver (1990) and Nelliapa (1992) who had shown that school environment played a significant role in differentiating Attitude towards Science in students. Based upon the result cited above, the investigator concluded that the result might be considered appropriate.

4.13 Analysis of Attitude Towards Science of Secondary School Students in Relation to School Success

The objective of the study was to determine the difference in Attitude towards Science of secondary

Table 4.13: Test of Significance of Difference on Attitude towards Science Scores due to School Success (High and Low Achieving Schools)

Variation	*Sub-Sample*	*N*	*M*	*SD*	*SED*	*'t'*	*Remark*
School success	High achieving	145	269.98	18.99	2.82	1.97	S
	Low achieving	95	264.42	23.12			

P values of t at 0.05 = 1.96, 0.01 = 2.58

school students in relation to school success i.e., high achieving schools and low achieving schools. In this respect, the investigator attempted to study the attitude of students of high achieving schools and low achieving schools taking into consideration the achievement of the school in the board examinations. So in order to test the tenability of hypothesis that there does not exist significant difference in the mean score of the students on Attitude towards Science in relation to differential levels of achievement variations, the 't' ratio was calculated and presented in Table 4.13.

From the Table 4.13, it was observed that the 't' ratio was 1.97 which was significant at 0.05 level. The result revealed that the mean attitude scores of students of high achieving schools were greater than the students of low achieving schools. Such a result clearly indicated that the high achieving schools have all types of facilities like teacher input, material input and process input for inculcating right type of attitude towards science in the students. The result was in conformity with earlier studies conducted by Raghavan (1991), Kar (1990) and Lin (1992) who had shown that school success played a significant role in differentiating attitude towards science in students. For further analysis of school success, the environmental conditions of the schools were determined on the basis of the scores obtained by the administration of the ISSEC of Parida (1994). The Information Schedule on School Environmental Condition (ISSEC) consists of three components namely, teacher input, material input and process input. The items distributed over three inputs were scored and a comparison was made in respect of the attitude towards science of students in relation to the three inputs. For this the differential analysis was made which were presented in the following pages. Out of 18 schools only 12 schools were identified as high achieving schools and only 6 schools as low achieving schools.

Table 4.14: Test of Significance of Difference between the Teacher Input of High and Low Achieving Schools (Both General and Professionals)

Category of Schools	*Number of Schools*	*I.A. / I.Sc. / C.T.*	*B.A. / B.Sc. / B.Ed. / M.Ed.*	*M.A. / M.Sc. / B.Ed. / M.Ed*
High Achieving Schools	12	14.3%	48.6%	27.6%
Low Achieving Schools	6	33.3%	41.5%	5.7%
Difference between percentage	D%	19	7.1	21.9
SD per cent	--	10.9	12.3	9.9
Critical Ratio (CR)	--	1.73	1.36	2.02
Levels of Significance	--	NS	NS	S

$P < 0.01$.

(a) Teacher Input in Schools and Attitude Towards Science

Teacher input was considered in respect of the qualification, experience, exposure to ideas and methods of teaching through participation in-service programmes. Tenability of hypothesis that there exists no significant difference in the percentage of teacher input of high and low achieving schools was tested. The result indicated that the teacher input in high achieving and low achieving schools was significant. The result was presented in Table 4.15.

A critical observation of the results and significance of difference between the percentages of high and low achieving schools in respect of different categories of teachers with general and professional qualification was made and it was observed that there was almost no significant difference. But a significant difference in distribution of teachers with M.A./M.Sc. with B.Ed./ M.Ed. qualification of high and low achieving schools had been found to be significant at 0.01 level. From the above findings the investigator desired to conclude that irrespective of nature of general and professional qualification of teachers the performance had been affected by professionally qualified teachers with B.Ed./ M.Ed. degree. Therefore the investigator desired to recommend minimum general qualification to be post-graduation with B.Ed. degree.

(b) Material Input in Schools and Attitude Towards Science

Effective teaching needs learning by doing and conceptualising the concept by the children themselves. So learning situations to be provided by the teachers must have adequate scope for performing certain activities for which learning materials are needed. In the present investigation the investigator sought for

Table 4.15: Test of Significance of Difference between the Material Input of High and Low Achieving Schools

Category of Schools	*Number of Schools (N)*	*Mean Score (MS)*	*S.D.*	*SED*	*'t'*	*P*
High Achieving Schools	12	30	4.1	2.87	5.574	0.01
Low Achieving Schools	6	14	6.4			

information for use of such materials in teaching-learning situations which promote effective learning and hence the attitude towards science of students was relatively high. So with this presumption in mind the investigator attempted to test the hypothesis that the material input of a school does not have any bearing upon the attitude towards science of the students. To test the tenability of such a hypothesis, the investigator attempted to examine if there existed any significant difference between the high and low achieving schools with regard to availability and use of materials. The data relating to the study of significance of difference between the high and low scoring schools in utilising different teaching materials was presented in Table 4.16.

The test of significance of difference in case of material input between high achieving schools and low achieving schools was found to be significant. Hence the null hypothesis that material input of a school did not have any bearing on the attitude towards science of the students was rejected. This provided a clue to the investigation that material input of a school had a vital role to play in pupil's attitude towards science.

(c) Process Input in Schools and Attitude Towards Science

The process input of each of the participating schools had also been quantified and calculated. As stated earlier there were eighteen participating schools, out of which twelve schools were high achieving schools and six were low achieving schools. The process input of these two categories of schools had been compared and tested for significance of differences in their mean scores in process input as per Garrett (1961). The result had been presented in Table 4.16.

A glance at the three Tables 4.14, 4.15, 4.16 revealed that teacher input, material input and process input in

Table 4.16: Test of Significance of Difference between High and Low Achieving Schools in Respect of Process Input

Category of schools	*Number of schools*	*Mean Score (MS)*	*S.D.*	*SED*	*'t'*	*P*
High Achieving Schools	12	26	1.7	0.78	19.23	0.01
Low Achieving Schools	6	11	1.5			

high and low achieving schools had significant differences in between them. Therefore, the null hypothesis formulated in this respect that the teacher input, material input and process input of a school does not affect the pupil's attitude towards science was rejected. It was also observed that there was glaring difference in the process input of high and low achieving schools for which it might be inferred that process input was a greater factor for inculcating attitude towards science in students.

4.14 Interaction Analysis

The interaction of independent variables like gender, socio-economic status and intelligence towards the dependent variable of attitude towards science were studied through two way analysis of variance. For this a design of 2x2x2 with two levels of gender, two levels of socio-economic status and two levels of intelligence were considered. The results were presented in a Table 4.17. The result obtained was considered to be appropriate in the context of the modern trend in urban areas, where parents of students spend enough money to educate their children in best schools in science streams.

On perusal of the Table 4.17, it was observed that main effect of gender and intelligence were significant at 0.01 level of significance but main effect of socio-economic status was not significant but the interaction effect of gender and intelligence was only significant leaving all others non-significant. This led to conclude that factors of gender and intelligence produced significant difference of Attitude towards Science of samples independently but the factor socio-economic status had not produced any significant difference of attitude towards science in students.

This result was supported by the findings of researchers like Ghosh (1990), Darchingpuii (1990),

Table 4.17: Summary of ANOVA Showing Interaction Effect on Attitude towards Science

Source of variation	*Sum of squares*	*Df*	*Mean square (MS)*	*F*	*Significance*
Gender	2924.062	1	2924.062	6.549	S $P < 0.01$
SES	421.638	1	421.638	0.944	NS
Intelligence	1975.431	1	1975.431	4.424	S $P < 0.05$
Gender XSES	712.415	1	712.415	1.956	NS
Gender X Intelligence	1850.145	1	1850.145	4.143	S $P < 0.05$
SES X Intelligence	552.232	1	552.232	1.236	NS
Gender X Intelligence X SES	1116.202	1	1116.202	2.499	NS
Error Variation	175030.073	392			

Alexander (1990), Nelliapa (1992), Raghavan (1991) and Ahamad, Raheem and Hasan (2003). From the Table 4.17, it was observed that the interaction between gender and socio-economic status on students' attitude towards science was not found significant (F ratio=1.956) which indicated that there was no significant interaction of gender and socio-economic status on students' attitude towards science. Hence the formulated null hypothesis HO_5 was accepted and concluded that there was no significant difference in attitude towards science of secondary school students in respect to combined impact of gender and socio-economic status.

Likewise the interaction between gender and intelligence on students' attitude towards science was found significant (F ratio = 4.143) which indicated that different levels of gender and intelligence interacted significantly on students' attitude towards science. Therefore, the null hypothesis HO_6 was rejected and concluded that there was significant difference in attitude towards science of secondary school students in respect to combined impact of gender and intelligence.

From the table, it was also observed that the interaction between socio-economic status and intelligence was not found significant (F ratio = 1.236) which indicated that different level of socio-economic status and intelligence did not interact significantly on students' attitude towards science. Therefore, the null hypothesis HO_7 was accepted and concluded that there was no significant difference in attitude towards science of secondary school students in respect to combined impact of socio-economic status and intelligence.

The interaction of gender, socio-economic status and intelligence on students' attitude towards science was not found significant (F ratio = 2.499) which indicated that different level of gender, socio-economic status and intelligence did not interact significantly on students' attitude towards science. Therefore, the null hypothesis HO_8 was accepted and concluded that there was no significant difference in attitude towards science of secondary school students in respect to triple impact of gender, socio-economic status and intelligence.

4.15 Analysis of Result in Respect of the Relationship between the Variables

Study of relationship between attitude towards science, socio-economic status and intelligence of the students were computed to find out the relationship between intelligence and socio-economic status as predicting variable to the criterion of Attitude towards Science. For this the Zero order co-efficient of correlation between socio-economic status, Intelligence and Attitude towards Science were calculated through Product Moment Correlation. In order to find out the contribution of socio-economic status and intelligence towards attitude towards science, the coefficient of multiple of correlation and multiple of coefficient determination (R^2) were computed by applying the appropriate formulae. The result was present in Table 4.18.

On perusal of the above table 4.18, it was observed that socio-economic status of whole sample had

Table 4.18: Zero Order Correlation between Socio-economic Status, Intelligence and Attitude towards Science

Variables	*SES*	*Intelligence*	*ATS*
SES	--	0.268**	0.423**
Intelligence	--	--	0.674**
ATS	--	--	--

** r = significant at 0.01 level of significance.

significant relationship with intelligence and attitude towards science. In order to find out relationship of the variables taken two at a time the coefficient of multiple correlation was computed for which the first order partial correlation of coefficient was calculated. The result was presented in table below:

Table 4.19: First Order Partial Correlation between Socio-economic Status, Intelligence and Attitude towards Science

Correlated Variables	*Symbol*	*Value*	*Significance Level*
ATS and SES Partialling out Intelligence	r 13.2	0.2349	0.01
SES and Intelligence Partialling out ATS	r 23.1	0.2012	0.01
ATS and Intelligence Partialling out SES	r 12.3	0.5371	0.01

From the table, it was observed that the relationship between attitude towards science and socio-economic status by partialling out intelligence was significant at 0.01 level of significance. The relationship between socio-economic status and intelligence by partialling out attitude towards science was also significant at 0.01 level of significance. The relationship between attitude towards science and intelligence by partialling out socio-economic status was also significant at 0.01 level of significance.

The coefficient of multiple correlation was calculated by applying the formula

$$R^2_{1.23} = 1- (1- r^2_{12}) (1-r_{13.2})^2$$

$$R_{13.2} = \frac{r_{13} - r_{12} \text{ X } r_{23}}{\text{Ö}1\text{-}r^2_{13} \; \text{Ö}1\text{-}r^2_{12}} \qquad \text{(Garrett, 2004, p. 453)}$$

And the result was found to be 0.376. This indicated that about 37.6 per cent of the variance due to socio-economic status and intelligence are contributed towards development of attitude towards science. Another 63 per cent variance might be attributed by other factors responsible for inculcating attitude towards science.

5

Summary and Recommendations

5.1 The Summary

Man's journey of life in this world is wonderful. Science is a journey towards the truth and we know that truth will make everybody fresh and free. Science has played key role in transforming the world from prehistoric age to the present age of globalisation. The boon and the curse of science, the world has experienced is well known to the present generation. The advancement of world in the field of agriculture, industry, health facility, education and other service sectors are all because of the development of science and technology. Today's booming global economy and the development of all nations in all walks of life is directly related to the development of science and technology. Science and technology are expanding at a fast rate and it has become the inseparable part of human activities. Now the life cannot be imagined without science and its products.

In the fast moving world and conflicting demand of the society, individual is faced with more and more problem that had made difficult to adjust. Therefore, there is a need for developing right sort of attitude to avoid any mental conflicts. One of the most important attitude that must be inculcated in students to make them useful and socially efficient citizens is the attitude towards science that can profitably developed through various subjects in general and in science subjects in particular. Because developing attitude towards science is potential means of eliminating intolerance, superstitions, obscurantism which are considered socially undesirable.

Rationale of the Study : Attitude towards science refers to an individual's outlook towards life. It means willingness to adopt scientific approaches and procedures for resolving issues/assessing ideas or information. Attitude towards science predisposes a person to engage in responsible action after weighing the possible consequences of alternative, options, using rational arguments based on evidence. She distinguishes between scientific evidence and personal opinion and between reliable and unreliable information, remains open to new evidence and the tentativeness of scientific knowledge and recognises that science and technology are human endeavours. Some other manifestations of the attitude towards science are questioning, suspension of judgement, appraisal of different sides of an issue, verification of knowledge, curiosity and appreciation of the natural and human made world, open mindedness, intellectual honesty, cooperation and tolerance of the point of view of other people. The attitude towards science presents a systematic account of the cognitive and social features of science.

Attitude towards science is compatible with observation and insight, reasoning and intuition, systematic work and creative impulse. It gives rise to an attitude of mind which while being conscious of vast areas of ignorance, is nevertheless, optimistic about human ability to gradually unravel the mysteries that surround us. In this process, attitude towards science becomes a part of the culture, a philosophy, and a way of life which leads to pursuit of truth without prejudgment. The inculcation of attitude towards science in our society would result in our people becoming rational and objective, thereby generating a climate favouring an egalitarian, democratic, secular and universalistic outlook. Social justice, widespread education and unrestricted communication are, therefore, pre-requisites for spread of attitude towards science and for optimising the results of science and technology. Mandila (1990) conducted a study on attitude of secondary stage student towards science curriculum and its relationship with achievement motivation. Sex and locale had favourable attitude towards science curriculum. There were significant differences in scientific temper. Bagchi (1993-94) studied the impact of different educational practices on student's attitude towards science. Ghosh (1990) found that parents' education and socio-economic status led to favourable attitude towards science beside other contributory factors. Thus, a clear cut picture of psychosocial variables influencing academic achievement had been there of research.

The present investigation was the noble attempt of the investigator in this area. Investigator was curious to determine, how students feel about science. The finding of this study might be seen as uncharacteristically positive, and not the least representative of previous research. Hence, the rationale of study is justified. Therefore, problem was stated as, "Attitude of secondary school students towards science in relation to some personal and institutional variables."

Objectives of the Study

The following objectives were formulated for the conduct of the study:

- To study the attitude towards science of secondary school students in relation to independent impact of variables (gender and socio-economic status);
- To study the difference in attitude towards science of secondary school students due to the personal variables of intelligence;
- To study the difference in attitude towards science of secondary school students due to some institutional variables like type of school, type of management, school environment and school success;
- To study the difference in attitude towards science of secondary school students in relation to combined impact of personal variables (gender and intelligence), (gender and socio-economic status) and (socio-economic status and intelligence);
- To find out the difference in attitude towards science in the secondary school students due to the interaction of gender, socio-economic status and intelligence.

Hypotheses of the Study

The hypotheses of the study were spelt out independently in null form for the ease of interpretation. They were:

Ho1: There is no significant difference in attitude towards science of the students in relation to gender variable.

Ho2: There is no significant difference in attitude towards science of secondary school students due to differential levels of Socio-economic Status.

Ho3: There exists no significant difference in attitude towards science of secondary school students in relation to differential levels of intelligence.

Ho4: There exists no significant difference in attitude towards science of secondary school students in relation to the institutional variables.

Ho5: There is no significant difference in attitude towards science of secondary school students in respect to combined impact of gender and socio-economic status.

Ho6: There is no significant difference in attitude towards science of secondary school students in respect to combined impact of gender and intelligence.

Ho7: There is no significant difference in attitude towards science of secondary school students in respect to combined impact of socio-economic status and intelligence.

Ho8: There is no significant difference in attitude towards science of secondary school students in respect to combined impact of the three variables of gender, socio-economic status and intelligence.

Delimitations of the Study

Only 10 per cent of the schools of Cuttack and Bhubaneswar city were selected at random out of 180 schools. A total sample of 400 responded for the study. The sample was taken from the same urbanised atmosphere of the twin cities in order to control the influence of any geographic variable.

Operational Definitions of the Terms

Attitude towards science: 'Attitude towards science' here refers to feelings, opinions, beliefs and appreciation which individuals have formed as a result of interacting directly or indirectly with the various aspects of the scientific enterprise.

Personal variables: 'Personal variables' here refer to gender, socio-economic status (SES) and intelligence.

Gender: 'Gender' here refers to the boys and girls.

Socio-economic Status: Socio-economic Status includes the information on education, occupation and income which determine the socio-economic status of the parents of the school children as measured by Nayak Socio-Economic Status scale (2005) and levels of Socio Economic Status have been considered under two levels i.e, high and low.

Intelligence: 'Intelligence' here refers to the general mental ability as measured by Group Test of General Mental Ability by Jalota (1971) and the levels of intelligence here also are categorised under high and low, as in case of Socio Economic Status. The categorisation of the levels of Socio Economic Status and Intelligence are made on the basis of mean (M) and Standard Deviation (SD) where higher than M + 1 SD relates to High level and less than M -1 SD is considered as the low level.

Institutional variables: 'Institutional variables' here refer to the type of management of institutions like government and non-government, boys and girls school, school success based on percentage of result in the final board examination and the school environmental facilities available to the students for studying science. The facilities can be categorised under two types i.e., schools having adequate and inadequate facilities. Therefore, the institutional variables may be studied under the following:

- **Type of management:** Government and Non-government managed schools.
- **Type of schools:** Boys, girls and co-educational schools.

- School Environment for studying science: Schools having adequate facilities, schools having inadequate facilities.
- School Success: It is here regarded by two levels like high achieving schools and low achieving schools making a cut off line of demarcation in percentage of results done in schools more than 75 per cent as high and less than 40 per cent as low in total.

The Method of the Study

The study was conducted in accordance with the following procedure:

The Design: In the present study, attitude of secondary school students towards science was studied in relation to gender, socio-economic status and intelligence and in relation to some institutional variables. Therefore, scores on students' attitude towards science were the criterion variables whereas gender, socio-economic status and intelligence were regarded as the predictive variables. Thus, it was primarily be a descriptive study design of ex-post facto nature.

The Sample: A representative sample consisting of 400 secondary school students were selected randomly from Cuttack and Bhubaneswar on simple random basis.

Tools Used: The tools used for this study were:

- Mishra's 2008 scale to measure Attitude towards Science.
- Group test of General Mental Ability by Jalota (1951) for assessing intelligence.
- Socio-Economic Status Scale of Nayak (2005) to determine the socio-economic background of students.

- Information Schedule on School Environmental Condition (ISSEC) developed by Parida (1994) to assess school environment climate.

Techniques of Data Analysis

The following techniques had been used for this study:

- Questioning technique was adopted for collection of data.
- The test of significance of difference (t) between the means of two contrasting sub-samples was adopted to find out significant difference.
- Each independent variable was to be considered under a factorial design of 2 x 2 x 2 with two levels of gender, Socio-Economic Status and Intelligence.
- Interactional Analysis among different levels of Gender, Socio-Economic Status and Intelligence was made through the technique of Analysis of variance (ANOVA).

5.2 Findings of the Study

After thorough study and data analysis, following findings had been noticed:

(i) There was significant difference in attitude towards science in boys and girls, girls outscoring the boys.

(ii) There was no significant difference between students of high socio-economic status and low socio-economic status in their attitude towards science.

(iii) There was significant difference between students of high intelligence and low intelligence on their attitude towards science.

(iv) There existed significant difference in the attitude towards science of secondary school students due to type of school management. Non-government schools students had high attitude towards science compared to students of government schools.

(v) There did not exist any significant difference in attitude towards science of secondary school students in relation to type of schools.

(vi) Students from schools having adequate facilities had better positive attitude towards science than students from schools having inadequate facilities.

(vii) There existed significant difference in the attitude towards science of secondary school students due to school success.

(viii) There existed significant difference between the high achieving schools and low achieving schools in case of teacher input, material input and process input for inculcating attitude towards science in students.

(ix) There did not exist significant difference in attitude towards science of secondary school students in respect to combined impact of gender and socio-economic status.

(x) There was significant difference in attitude towards science of secondary school students in respect to combined impact of gender and intelligence.

(xi) There did not exist any significant difference in attitude towards science of secondary school students in respect to combined impact of socio-economic status and intelligence.

(xii) There did not exist any significant difference in attitude towards science of secondary school students in respect to interaction effect of gender, socio-economic status and intelligence.

(xiii) Socio-economic status of whole sample had significant relationship with intelligence and attitude towards science.

(xiv) The relationship between attitude towards science and socio-economic status by partialling out intelligence was significant.

(xv) The relationship between socio-economic status and intelligence by partialling out attitude towards science was significant.

(xvi) The relationship between attitude towards science and intelligence by partialling out socio-economic status was significant.

5.3 The Recommendations

In this study the focus was on the student's attitude towards science. Perhaps it might be useful to get some feedback from the science teachers and school administrators to support the student's data. Such a study can look at the attitude of lower secondary schools students towards science. In this way, the study would not be confined to a group of students only and more information can be obtained about student's attitude from different levels in the secondary schools.

After a study of attitude towards science of secondary school students, the following measures were recommended for its improvement.

Requisites for an Effective Science Teacher: A secondary school science teacher is required to have a post graduate degree in science to meet the requirement of present day science curriculum. In-service teacher training should be compulsory for all science teachers. A teacher must attend an orientation course once in every five years to refresh his/her knowledge in content as well as technique of teaching. Every teacher should be trained to inculcate attitude towards science in his/her students by helping them to apply their own minds instead of rote learning. Teachers are to be motivated to conduct action research programme and make use of result in the working situation.

Role of a Science Teacher : The major role can be played by the science teacher in developing attitude towards science among his students and this he can do by manipulating various situations that infuse among the pupils certain characteristics of attitude towards science. He can also help in developing attitude towards science among his students if he possesses and practices various elements of these attitudes. The practical examples given by the teacher leaves an indelible mark on the personality of his students. Teacher can use one or more of the ways for developing attitude towards science among his pupils.

Inculcation of Attitude Towards Science through Curricular and Co-curricular Practices

A large number of exercises for development of certain attitude towards science are reported by various journals and magazines. Teachers can frequently use such exercises for developing certain attitude towards science among the pupils. He can also make use of cuttings from newspapers and science magazines and can display such materials on bulletin board so that it is used again and again for direct teaching. Exercises which are always included in good text books can also be used by the teacher for developing attitude towards science among his pupils. A teacher should encourage his students to read library books and supplementary books on science. For this it is essential that each school at least has a science corner in its library. The teacher himself must be in habit of making proper use of science library so that his students get encouragement for use of science library. The teacher himself be familiar with the latest new titles in his subject and he willing to share his joys of new readings with his pupils. He should refer some suitable books to his students.

Proper Use of Practical Period: A student of science gets many opportunities for learning attitudes towards science during his practical periods. It is for the teacher to properly use such opportunities for developing attitudes towards science amongst his pupils. Teacher should take extra care to state the problem of the experiment and should present hypotheses on solution. He should practice the proper method of testing the hypothesis. He should actively participate in discussion and interpretation of results after the experiment. He must inculcate in his students the habit to postpone judgements in the absence of sufficient evidence to support a hypothesis. He must inculcate in his students scientific attitude, scientific technique and understanding through heuristic lines.

Infrastructure Facilities

- ***Laboratory:*** A laboratory cum science room is the basic requirement of the school. Steps in this direction should be taken. In science room charts, diagrams, graphs are to be displayed, fixed and laboratory equipments and chemicals are to be stored as per requirement.

- ***Library:*** Attention must be given to update library condition keeping in view of the needs of students and teachers. There should be reference books, magazine, journals for updating teacher's knowledge. Science books can be kept in general library but its importance should be realised by the students and teachers.

Teaching Learning Process

- ***Method of teaching:*** The different methods to be practiced in school are (i) Lecture method, (ii) demonstration method, (iii) lecture cum demonstration method, (iv) observation method, (v) problem solving method, (vi) project method, (vii) heuristic method, (viii) laboratory method, (ix) assignment method etc. Out of all the methods, lecture cum demonstration, observation cum discussion methods are very much recommended for science teaching.

- ***Audio Visual Aids in Teaching:*** Now it is recommended that the audio visual aids like TV, Cassette recorder, projectors, cinematography, VCR and radio sets should be provided in each school. Through these the demonstrations to the students are made more attractive, acceptable, lively and understandable. The students not only easily comprehend the content but also able to remember it better for longer duration. The creative potentiality of the child is also enhanced from it.

Science Fairs, Exhibitions and Science Club Activities

Every school should organise science fairs at least once a year. The programme should include exhibits prepared by students. Talks by experts, film shows on scientific topics debate and discussion, music shows, scientific plays, quiz, etc., can also be organised. Both the teachers and pupils should cooperate and contribute towards the success of such fairs. Every school must encourage science club activities and these activities are to be assessed at state level.

Science Museum

It is much desirable that every school should have a science museum of its own. The science teacher should encourage the student to collect materials of scientific interest and improvise some apparatus. The collection of materials relating to different branches of science and a systematic arrangement of the same should be on the basis of a co-operative and active endeavour of the teachers and the students alike.

Excursion and Tours

Learning in the classroom cannot be sufficient for a student of modern time. So excursion and visits and field trips to different places of scientific importance should be organised annually to given an opportunity to the participants to get direct and practical learning experiences in an interesting manner. Science teacher must arrange tours to radio station, telephone exchange, gardens, factories, planetarium which will supplement class-room instruction. The science teacher must advise the students to collect information and note them accurately for their study to develop the habit of correct observation and recording.

Modification of Science Syllabus

Science syllabus needs to be thoroughly revised and new topics are to be included taking into consideration of the resources available in the schools and the needs of children in every three years.

Upgradation of the Text Books

The review of existing text books is felt very essential. Workshops are to be organised to develop suitable text books and agencies like NCERT, SCERT, etc. should take leadership in this regard. Both working teachers and subject expert need to be involved in the programme of upgrading text book.

Provision of Wall Magazines on Topic of Scientific Interest

Students must be inspired to participate in creating and reading wall magazines with inspiring success stories in science and technology.

Improvement of the Quality of Science Education

Continuous efforts are being carried out by the science educators and experts to improve the quality of science education and teacher training in the light of the changing needs of the child and society and the changing nature of the subject matter, but it has not gained momentum. Even after these strenuous efforts to improve the quality of science education and training, which have to do a lot.

In this context, it will be worthwhile if some ideas are placed before the educationists for open discussion to improve the quality of science education in secondary schools.

- The curriculum must be need-based.
- Curriculum should develop attitude towards science and decisions making power.
- Content organisation must consider the contemporary scientific knowledge.
- Curriculum should consider various age-groups, sex and I.Q. levels.
- Curriculum must bring certain learning (productive) outcomes in its pursuers in the domains cognitive, affective and psychomotor in order to find a place in the world of work.
- Emphasis should be given to the acquisition of abilities in affective and psychomotor fields.
- Emphasis must be given to learning of concepts rather than to acquisition of information.
- Curriculum should be child-centred.
- Curriculum should encourage interdisciplinary approach.

- Environmental resources should be utilised.
- Curriculum must bring awareness in the thrust area like health, nutrition, shelter, environment, agriculture, energy, wildlife, social forestry, industry, human welfare, ecological balance, etc.
- Learning outcomes must be properly evaluates.
- Provision must be made for practical work.
- Schools should be adequately equipped with library, laboratory and physical facilities.
- Schools should acquire the necessary audio visual materials either professionally made or improvised, but they should not sacrifice the accuracy of science in the name of zero cost or low cost aids.
- The teachers, as earlier stated, are the only instruments to impart quality education, hence, their pre-service and in-service training must be strengthened.
- Teacher must be enriched in content and methodology.
- Teacher should be made aware of the concept of scientific literacy.
- Children should be involved intensively in learning.
- Science education must reach the out of school children through non-formal agencies.
- Teacher educators have to find out the thrust area, identify the drawbacks, develop feasible procedures to practice them in both training colleges and schools.
- Teacher educators, the key agents of change, can easily mould their student clientele up to the mark,

in turn the products will put into practice the advantageous teaching techniques and ideas to upgrade the children's consciousness of science, its importance and its impact on day to day life.

The sole responsibility of developing attitude towards science among the students lies on the teachers who can manipulate a variety of situations to in-still in pupils the characteristic features of attitude towards science, and at the same time present themselves as an example to the students for their intellectual honesty, respect for others point of views, unbiased and impartial behaviours in their dealings and the like. Many transactional strategies have been evolved and suggested to develop attitude towards science. Some of them are the outcome of elaborate efforts of researches. The teacher should use constructivist approach of teaching and learning and facilitate learners to reflect, analyse, and interpret in the process of knowledge, construction. Students should be trained in scientific method. They should be posed with certain situations to be solved by them by using scientific method only. The curriculum should be such which promotes honesty, objectivity, co-operation, freedom from fear and prejudice, and develops in the learner a concern for life and preservation of environment. Emphasis should be given on experiments and problem-solving, discovery approach, enquiry approach, hemistich approach, and other approaches of teaching and learning which are based on principle of learning by doing and self-driver learning. Science curriculum should be oriented more towards developing awareness among the learners about the interface of science, technology and society, sensitising them especially to the issues of environment and health and enabling them to acquire practical knowledge and skills to enter the world of work. It should stress not only the content of science but also, more importantly, the process skills of science, that is, the method and techniques of learning science. This is essential since the process skills are more enduring and enable the learner to cope with the ever changing and expanding field of science and technology. As far as possible, teachers should try to discuss the social implications of the content being taught to the students to sensitise them. For example, co-operation may be taught through covalent bond, sacrifice and co-existence through electrovalent bond and co-ordination through co-ordinate bond. When we are teaching air as a mixture of gases; we can relate by saying that air contains so many gases in different amounts. Some are in very high amount, some moderate and some in traces. All have their own importance. Similarly, human societies are rich and poor, white and black, high caste and low caste, and all of them should be treated well. There should not be any discrimination on any ground. Thus, a well-designed emphasis is required on all the three aspects – content, process, and value orientation. If attitude towards science is inculcated among our learners, they can solve all their problems in a scientific manner be it a personal problem, family problem, social problem or problems of any level or any kind. In addition to the reformation in the pedagogical aspects, the evaluation system also needs to be reformed.

There should be well defined procedure of internal evaluation and specially the teacher should assess the attitude towards science and valued being inculcated among the learners and should grade them and this grade should be made a decisive criteria for higher education, other professional courses and in getting employment.

5.4 Implications for Further Research

Researches are never complete. One research opens various new directions for further researchers and this way knowledge expands. The present investigation also abides by the same rule. This study has given rise to many problems for further researches. The present study opens up certain avenues for further research, which are:

- The present study can be replicated in different parts of the country with large sample and with students of various age groups.
- The present study can be replicated on a large and more representative sample, so that the result obtained may be more reliable.
- Similar studies can be conducted on the primary school, middle school and university students.
- The study of the same nature can be undertaken for the different states of the country.
- A similar study can be conducted by taking into consideration other variables such as Achievement in Science, Aptitude in Science, Science Reasoning etc.
- A comparative study of relationship between Sex, SES and Intelligence on attitude towards science can be undertaken among students of different states and different countries.
- A number of studies are also needed to evaluate the effectiveness of teachers in terms of their attitude towards science and science teaching and their understanding of nature of science.
- A teachers training programme should also be evaluated in terms of development of understanding of nature of science as well as interests and attitude towards science teaching through discovery approach.

Bibliography

Ahmad, J. (2008). Scientific Attitude: Solution to all problems. *School Science, NCERT,* New Delhi, Vol. 46. No. 4, 41-42.

Ahamed, N., Raheem, A. and Hasan, A. (2003). Attitude of Secondary School Students towards Science in Relation to Sex, Socio-economic Status and Intelligence. *Indian Educational Review,* Vol. 39,(2) 80-89.

Alexander, B. (1990). A Study of Critical Thinking, Science Aptitude and Socio-Economic Status to the Science Achievement of Second Year P.U.C. Students. *Fifth Survey of Educational Research,* Vol. I, 361.

Allport, G. W. (1935). Attitude. In Fishbein, M.(ed). Reading in Attitude Theory and Measurement. New York: John Wiley and Sons, 1-13.

Alwis, C. D. (2004). Attitude of From Two Student's Toward Learning Science in English: A Case Study of Schools in Kota Samarshan. University Technology MARA Sarawak.

Askwall, C. and Hermanson, K. (2007). Young People Attitudes towards Science and Researchers. Vetenskap and All Manhet, VA, Stockholm, Sweden.

Aikenhead, G. (1995). *Cultural Assimilation in Science Classrooms: Border Crossings and Other Solutions*. Unpublished paper.

Aikenhead, G., Ryan, A. G. and Fleming, R. W. (1989). *Views on Science–technology–Society* (Saskatoon, Saskatchewan: Department of Curriculum Studies).

Ajzen, I. and Fishbein, M. (1980). *Understanding Attitudes and Predicting Social Behaviour* (Englewood Cliffs, NJ: Prentice Hall).

Archer, J. (1992). Gender Stereotyping of School Subjects. *The Psychologist,* 5, 66–69.

Baker, D. and Leary, R. (1995). Letting Girls Speak out about Science. *Journal of Research in Science Teaching*, 32, 3–27.

Barnett, C. (2001). *Prelude to an Industrial Defeat from the 1944 Education Act to the 1956 White Paper on Technological Education* (London: Royal Society of Arts).

Beaton, A., Martin, M. O., Mullis, I., Gonzalez, E. J., Smith, T. A. and Kelley, D. L. (1996). *Science achievement in the middle school years: IEA's Third International Mathematics and Science Study* (Chestnut Hill, MA: Boston College).

Becker, B. J. (1989). Gender and science achievement: analysis of studies from two meta-analyses. *Journal of Research in Science Teaching*, 26, 141–169.

Bennett, J. (2001). The development and use of an instrument to assess students' attitude to the study of chemistry. *International Journal of Science Education*, 23, 833–845.

Bergin, D. A. (1999). Influences on classroom interest. *Educational Psychologist*, 34, 87–98.

Breakwell, G. M. and Beardsell, S. (1992). Gender, parental and peer influences upon science attitudes and activities. *Public Understanding of Science*, 1, 183–197.

Brown, S. (1976). *Attitude Goals in Secondary School Science* (Stirling: University of Stirling).

Boone, W. J. (1997). Science Attitudes of Selected Middle School Students in China: A Preliminary Investigation of Similarities and Differences as a Function of Gender. *School Science and Mathematics,* 97(2), 96-103.

Bricheno, P. (2000). Science Attitude Changes on Transition. *Paper presentation at the ASE Conference, Leeds.*

Barton, A. C. (2000). Crafting Multicultural Science Education with Pre-service Teachers through Service-Learning, *Journal Curriculum Studies,* 32, 6, 797-820.

Bagchi, J. P. (1993-94). Student's Attitude Towards Science: The Impact of Different Educational Practices. *Journal of Indian Education,* Vol. XIX (4-5), 50-56.

Bhagwat, S. (2006). Manual for Scientific Attitude Scale, *National Psychological Corporation, Agra, 1-6.*

Campbell, B. (2001). Children' Perceptions of Science Education at Primary and Secondary School, in: Behrendt, H: Dahncke, H.et al (2001) Research in Science Education Past, Present and Future. London, Kluwer Academic Publishers.

Crawley, F. E. and Koballa, T. R. (1994). Attitude Research in Science Education, *Science Education,* 78, 35-55.

Collis, B. and Williams, R. (1990). Cross Cultural Comparison of Gender Differences in Adolescents' Attitudes Toward Computers and Selected School

Subjects. *The Journal of Educational Research,* 81 (1), 17-27.

Chun-yen C. (2008). Science Achievement and Student's Self Confidence and Interest in Science: *A Taiwan Representative Sample Study.*

Chauhan, D. (2008). Attitude of Secondary School Students towards Science in Relation to Institutional Variables. *Unpublished Thesis in Education, University of North Bengal.*

Cannon, R. K. and Simpson, R. D. (1990). Relationships Among Attitude, Motivation and Achievement of Ability Grouped, Seventh-Grade and Life Science Students. *Science Education,* 69,121-138.

Cruzel, H. (2004). The Relationship between Students' Success in Physics Lessons and Their Attitudes towards Mathematics. *Journal of Turkish Science Education,* Vol.1, July. 36-38.

Cheng, Y., Payne, J. and Witherspoon, S. (1995). *Science and Mathematics in Full-time Education after 16: England and Wales Youth Cohort Study* (London: Department for Education and Employment).

Colley, A., Comber, C. and Hargreaves, D. (1994). School subject preference of pupils in single sex and co-educational secondary schools. *Educational Studies*, 20, 379–386.

Cooper, P. and Mcintyre, D. (1996). *Effective teaching and learning: teachers' and students' perspectives* (Buckingham: Open University Press).

Cossons, N. (1993). Let us take science into our culture. *Interdisciplinary Science Reviews*, 18, 337–342.

Crawley, F. E. and Black, C. B. (1992). Causal modelling of secondary science students intentions to enrol in physics. *Journal of Research in Science Teaching*, 29, 585–599.

Crawley, F. E. and Coe, A. E. (1990). Determinants of middle school students' intentions to enrol in a high school science course: an application of the theory of reasoned action. *Journal of Research in Science Teaching*, 27, 461–476.

Dearing, R. (1996). *Review of Qualifications for 16–19 year old* (London: Schools Curriculum and Assessment Authority).

De Boer, G. (2000). Scientific literacy: another look at its historical and contemporary meanings and its relationship to science education reform. *Journal of Research in Science Teaching*, 37, 582–601.

Dillon, J., Osborne, J., Fairbrother, R. and Kurina, L. (2000). *A study into the professional views and needs of science teachers in primary and secondary schools in England* (London: King's College London).

Doherty, J. and Dawe, J. (1988). The relationship between development maturity and attitude to school science. *Educational Studies*, 11, 93–107.

Donnelly, J. (2001). Contested terrain or unified project? 'The nature of science' in the National Curriculum for England and Wales. *International Journal of Science Education*, 23, 181–195.

Durant, J. and Bauer (1997). *Public understanding of science: the 1996 survey*. Paper presented at a seminar at the Royal Society, 8 December 1997.

Durant, J. R., Evans, G. A. and Thomas, G. P. (1989). The public understanding of science. *Nature*, 340, 11–14.

Dweck, C. S. (1986). Motivational processes affecting learning. *American Psychologist*, 41, 1040–1048.

Dweck, C. S. and Leggett, E. L. (1988). A social-cognitive approach to motivation and personality. *Psychological Review*, 95, 256–273.1076

Defiana, A. (1995). Environmental Awareness: Relating Current Issues to Biology. *The Science Teachers,* 21: 37-39.

Dunlop, M. and Catherine, S. (2004). Perceptions of the Learning Environment, Attitudes Towards Science and Understandings of the Nature of Science among Prospective Elementary Teachers in an Innovative Science Course. *Ph.D. Dissertation, Curtin University.*

Darchingpuii (1990). A Study of Science Achievement, Science Attitude and Problem-solving Attitude among the Secondary School Students in Aizawal. *Fifth Survey of Educational Research.* Vol.I, 361.

Dorman, J. P., Fisher, D. L. and Waldrip, B. G. (2007). Classroom Environment, Students' Perceptions of Assessment, Academic Efficacy and Attitude towards Science: *A Lisrel Analysis. University of Southern Queensland, Australia.*

Dorman, J. P. (2002). Classroom Environment Research: Progress and Possibilities. *Queensland Journal of Educational Research,* 18,112-140.

Dubey, K. K. (1992). A Study of the Scientific Temper and its Measurement, Ph. D., Educ. *Rani Durgawati Vishwavidyalaya.Fifth Survey of Educational Research.*Vol.1, 360.

Dhinsa, H. S. and Chung, C. (2003). Attitudes and Achievements of Brunei Science Students. *International Journal of Science Education,* 23, 213-215.

Edwards, A. L. (1957). Techniques of Attitude Scale Construction. *New York. Appleton Century Corfts Inc.*

Engstrom, J. and Noonan, R. (1990). Science Achievement and Attitudes in Swedish Schools. *Studies in Educational Evaluation,* 16, 443-456

Ebnezer, J. V. and Zoller, N. (1993). Grade 10 Student's Perception of the Attitude towards Science Teaching and School Science. *Journal of Research in Science Teaching,* 30,175-186.

Eccles, J. S. (1987). Gender roles and women's achievement related decisions. *Psychology of Women Quarterly*, 11, 135–171.

Eccles, J. S. and Wigfield, A. (1992). The development of achievement-task values: a theoretical analysis. *Developmental Review*, 12, 265–310.

Eccles, J. S. and Wigfield, A. (1995). In the mind of the actor: the structure of adolescents' achievement task values and expectancy-related beliefs. *Personality and Social Psychology Bulletin*, 21, 215–225.

Education Policies Commission (1962). *Education and the spirit of science* (Washington, DC: Education Policies Commission).

Elwood, J. and Comber, C. (1995). *Gender differences in 'A' level examinations: the reinforcement of stereotypes*. Paper presented as part of the symposium A New Era? New contexts for gender equality: BERA conference, 11–13, September.

Epstein, J. L. and Mcpartland, J. M. (1976). The concept and measurement of the quality of school life. *American Educational Research Journal*, 13, 15–30.

Erickson, G. and Erickson, L. (1984). Females and science achievement: evidence, explanations and implications. *Science Education*, 68, 63–89.

Fielding, H. (1998). *The undesirable choices?* Unpublished. London: King's College London.

Fraser, B. J. (1982). How strongly are attitude and achievement related? *School Science Review*, 63, 557–559.

Fraser, B. J. (1986). *Classroom environment* (London: Croom Helm).

Fisher & Koul, R. B. (2004). Students' Perception of Science Leaving Environment in Jammu; Attitudes and Gender Differences. *Indian Journal of Science Communication,* Vol. 3 (2), 16-25.

Fraser, B. J. (1998). Science Learning Environments: Assessments, Effects and Determinants. In B.J. Fraser and K.G.Tobin (Eds.), *International Handbook of Science Educational, Dordrecht, The Netherlands: Kluwer,* 527-564.

Garrett, H. E. (1961). Statistics in Psychology and Education. Published by Paragon International Publishers, New Delhi. Reprint in 2004,388-391,453.

Ghosh, S. (1990). A Critical Study of Scientific Attitude and Aptitude of the Students and Determination of Some Determinants of Scientific Attitude. *In* M.B.Butch (Edited) *Fourth Survey of Educational Research,* Vol. 1,715.

Ghosh, S. (1990). A Critical Study of Scientific Attitude and Aptitude of the Students and Determination of Some Determinants of Scientific Attitude. Ph.D., Edu. *University of Kalyani, Fifth Survey of Educational Research.* Vol.1, 360.

Gautam, V. (2002). A study of Attitude towards Science in Relation to Interest in Science. *Researches and Studies,* Vol. 46-53, 87-89.

Gakhar, S. C. and Kaur, A. (2004). Manual for Scientific Attitude Scale. Published by Rakhi Prakashan, Agra , 3-5.

Grewal, A. (1990). Manual for Scientific Attitude Scale. Published by National Psychology Corporation, Agra, 2-4.

Guilford, J. P. (1965). *Fundamental Statistics in Psychology and Education.* 4th Ed.; New York: McGraw-Hill Book Co., 267-269.

Gardner, P. L. (1975). Attitudes to science. *Studies in Science Education*, 2, 1–41.

Gardner, P. L. (1995). Measuring attitudes to science. *Research in Science Education*, 25, 283–289.

Gauld, C. F. and Hukins, A. A. (1980). Scientific attitudes: a review. *Studies in Science Education*, 7, 129–161.

Gogolin, L. and Swartz, F. (1992). A quantitative and qualitative inquiry into the attitudes toward science of non-science college majors. *Journal of Research in Science Teaching*, 29, 487–504.

Greenfield, T. A. (1995). Sex-differences in Science Museum exhibit attraction. *Journal of Research in Science Teaching*, 32, 925–938.

Hadden, R. A. and Johnstone, A. H. (1983). Secondary school pupils' attitudes to science: the year of erosion. *European Journal of Science Education*, 5, 309–318.

Haladyna, T.,Olsen, R. and Shaughnessy, J. (1982). Relations of student, teacher, and learning environment variables to attitudes to science. *Science Education*, 66, 671–687.

Harding, J. (1983). *Switched off: the science education of girls* (New York: Longman).

Harding, S. (1991). *Whose science? Whose knowledge?* (Ithaca, NY: Cornell University Press).

Harvey, T. J. and Edwards, P. (1980). Children's expectations and realisations of science. *British Journal of Educational Psychology*, 50, 74–76.

Haskell, J. and Martin, C. (1994). *Will skill shortages end the recovery* (London: Department of Economics, Queen Mary College).

Havard, N. (1996). Student attitudes to studying A-level sciences. *Public Understanding of Science,* 5(4), 321–330.

Head, J. O. (1985). *The personal response to science* (Cambridge: Cambridge University Press).

Hendley, D., Parkinson, J., Stables, A. and Tanner, H. (1995). Gender differences in pupil attitudes to the national curriculum foundation subjects of English, mathematics, science and technology in Key Stage 3 in South Wales. *Educational Studies*, 21, 85–97.

Hendley, D., Stables, S. and Stables, A. (1996). Pupils' subject preferences at Key Stage 3 in South Wales. *Educational Studies*, 22, 177–187.

Hidi, S. (2000). Motivating the academically unmotivated. *Review of Educational Research*, 7, 151–179.

Hendley, D. (1995). *Gender Differences in Pupil Educational Studies.* Vol. 21, 1, 85-97.

Harty, H. and Samuel, K. V. (1990). Exploring Relationships among Four Science Teaching-Learning Effectives Attributes of Sixth Grade Students. *Journal of Research in Science Teaching,* 23, 51-60.

Hasan, O. E. and Bilch, V. Y. (1975). Relationship between Teacher's Change in Attitudes towards Science and Some Professional Variables. *Journal of Research in Science Teaching,* 12, 155-261.

Johnston, J., Mckcown, E., Cowan, P., Mccline, B. and Mcewen, A. (1999). What Science Engenders: Boys, Girls and the Teaching and Learning of Primary Science. Belfast, *Equal Opportunities Commission for Northern Ireland.*

Jayasree, K. (1998). Socialisation Ability, Scientific Attitude towards Science in Junior College Student – A Study. *Unpublished Doctoral Dissertation, Nagarjuna University. Sixth Survey of Educational Research,* Vol.1. 84.

Jenkins, E. W. (1994). Public understanding of science and science education for action. *Journal of Curriculum Studies*, 26, 601–612.

Johnson, S. (1987). Gender differences in science: parallels in interest, experience and performance. *International Journal of Science Education*, 9, 467–481.

Jones, G., Howe, A. and Rua, M. (2000). Gender differences in students' experiences, interests, and attitudes towards science and scientists. *Science Education*, 84, 180–192.

Jovanoic, J. and King, S. S. (1998). Boys and girls in the performance-based science classroom: who's doing the performing? *American Educational Research Journal*, 35, 477–496.

Kahle, J. B. and Lakes, M. K. (1983). The myth of equality in science classrooms. *Journal of Research in Science Teaching*, 20, 131–140.

Kahneman, D. and Tversky, A. (1984). Choices, values, and frames. *American Psychologist*, 39, 341–350.

Keller, E. F. (1985). *Reflections on gender and science* (New Haven, CT: Yale University Press).

Kennedy, P. (1993). *Preparing for the twenty-first century* (New York: Random House).

Keys, W. (1987). *International studies in pupil performance: aspects of science education in English schools* (Windsor: NFER-Nelson).

Kingsland, R. (1991). Science clubs – the extra dimension. *International Journal of Science Education*, 13, 589–596.

Klopfer, L. E. (1971). Evaluation of learning in science. In B. S. Bloom, J. T. Hastings and G. F. Madaus (Eds.), *Handbook of formative and summative evaluation of student learning* (London: McGraw-Hill).

Koballa Jr., T. R. (1988). The determinants of female junior high school students' intentions to enrol in elective physical science courses in high school: testing the applicability of the theory of reasoned action. *Journal of Research in Science Teaching*, 25, 479–492.

Koballa Jr., T. R. (1995). Children's attitudes toward learning science. In S. Glyyn and R. Duit (Eds.), *Learning science in the schools* (Mawhah, NJ: Lawrence Erlbaum).

Koballa, T. R. (1990). Attitude and Related Concepts in Science Education. *Science Education,* 72(2), 115-126.

Kar, D. K. (1990). A Study of Relationship between Attitude towards and Achievement in General Science of Class IX Students of Cuttack City. *Fifth Survey of Educational Research,* Vol. I, 361.

Khatoon, T. (1998). Minority Student's Attitude towards Science and their Achievement: A Comparative Study. *Indian Educational Review,* 170-177.

Koballa, T. R. (1990). Changing and Measuring Attitude in the Classroom, Research Matters to the Science Teacher, *National Association for Research in Science Teaching.*

Kumar, U. (1991). The Teaching of General Science and the Development of Scientific Attitude in Secondary

School Students in Relation to Achievement in General Science. *Fifth Survey of Educational Research,* Vol. 1, 360.

Kozlow, M. J. and Nay, M. A. (1974). An Approach to Measuring Scientific Attitude. *Science Education,* 147-172.

Karthikeyan, M. and Mohideen, S. R. (2005). A Study of Correlation between the Availability and Utilisation of Physics Laboratory Facilities in Higher Secondary Schools and Attitude of Higher Secondary Students towards Physics Practical. *Journal of Education Research and Extension,* Vol. 42 (2), 35-47.

Lemke, J. (2001). Articulating communities: sociocultural perspectives on science education. *Journal of Research in Science Teaching*, 38, 296–316.

Lepkowska, D. (1996). The non-appliance of science. *Evening Standard*, 3 September, 33–34.

Lightbody, P. and Durnbell, A. (1996). Gendered career choice: is sex-stereotyping the cause or the consequence. *Educational Studies*, 22, 133–146.

Lightbody, P. and Durnbell, A. (1996). The masculine image of careers in science and technology – fact or fantasy. *British Journal of Educational Psychology*, 66, 231–246.

Lightbody, P., Siann, G., Stocks, R. and Walsh, D. (1996). Motivation and attribution at secondary school: the role of gender. *Educational Studies*, 22, 13–25.

Lin, H. S. (1998). Enhancing College Students' Attitudes towards Science thought the History of Science. National Kaohsiung Normal University, Koohsiuhg, R.O.C., *Proc.Natt .sci-coumc. Roc (D),* Vol. 8, No. 2, 86-91.

Lama, P. D. (2010). Achievement in Science in relation to Attitude towards Science at the Secondary Level. *Unpublished Thesis in Education, Sikkim Central University.*

Likert, R. (1932). A Technique for the Measurement of Attitude. *Archives of Psychology.* Vol. 140. 24-28.

Lin, H. S. (1992). Trend Analysis and Prediction of Students' Science Attitude and Achievement in Taiwan, Republic of China. Unpublished Doctoral Dissertation, University of Minnesota, Minneapolis, MN.

Lalitha, P. R. and Lakshminarayan, V. (2002). Study of Attitude of +2 Students towards Physics Laboratory Work. *School Science,* Vol.40 (2), June, 45-53.

Maitra, K. and Maitra, A. (1997). To Explore the Attitude Towards Laboratories and Other Related Practical Work in Science. *Fifth Survey of Educational Research,* Vol. I, 84.

Malviya, D. S. (1991). A Study of Attitude towards Science and Interest in Science of School Going Adolescents. *Fifth Survey of Educational Research,* Vol. I, 360.

Mandila, S. S. (1990). Attitude of Secondary Stage Students towards Science Curriculum and its Relationship with Achievement-Motivation. *Fifth Survey of Educational Research,* Vol. I, 360.

Mishra, S. (2011). Relationship between Reasoning Ability in and Attitude towards Science of the students at the secondary level. *Himalayan Journal of Social Sciences,*Vol.1, No.1,17-23.

Munby, H. (1983). Thirty Studies Involving the Scientific Attitude Inventory: What Confidence Can We have in this Instrument. *Journal of Research in Science Teaching,* 20, 141-162.

Myers, R. E. and Fouts, J. T. (1992). A cluster Analysis of High School Science Classroom Environments and Attitude towards Science. *Journal of Research in Science Teaching*. 29, 929-937.

Moon, S. M. (1994). The Relationship among Gender, Computer Experience and Attitude towards Computers. *Annual Meeting of the Mid-South Educational Research Association, Nashville USA, Nov. 9-11.*

Mason, C. L., and Kahle, J. B. (1990). Student's Attitude towards Science-related Careers. A Program Designing to Promote a Stimulating Gender Free Learning Environment, *Journal of Research in Science Teaching,* 26, 25-39.

Mordi, C. (1991). Factors Associated with Pupils' Attitudes towards Science in Nigerian Primary Schools. *Research in Science and Technological Education,* 9, 39-49.

Mcewen, A., Curry, C. A. and Watson, J. (1986). Subject preferences at A level in Northern Ireland. *European Journal of Science Education*, 8, 39–49.

Mcmillan, J. H. and May, M. J. (1979). A study of the factors influencing attitudes toward science of junior high school students. *Journal of Research in Science Teaching*, 16, 217–222.

Mead, M. and Metraux, R. (1957). Image of the scientist among high-school students. *Science*, 126, 384–390.

Millar, M. G. and Tesser, A. (1986). Effects of affective and cognitive focus on the attitude– behaviour relation. *Journal of Personality and Social Psychology*, 51, 270–276.

Millar, M. G. and Tesser, A. (1989). The effects of affective and cognitive focus on the attitude–behaviour relation. *Journal of Experimental Social Psychology*, 25, 189–202.

Miller, J. D., Pardo, R. and Niwa, F. (1997). *Public perceptions of science and technology: a comparative study of the European Union, the United States, Japan, and Canada* (Bilbao: BBV Foundation).

Modood, T. (1993). The number of ethnic minority students in higher education. Some ground for optimism. *Oxford Review of Education*, 19, 167–182.

Moore, R. W. and Sutman, F. X. (1970). The development, field test and validation of an inventory of scientific attitudes. *Journal of Research in Science Teaching*, 7, 85–94.

Munro, M. and Elsom, D. (2000). *Choosing science at 16: the influences of science teachers and careers advisors on students' decisions about science subjects and science and technology careers* (Cambridge: Careers Research and Advisory Centre).

Murphy, C. and Beggs, J. (2001). *Pupils' attitudes, perceptions and understanding of primary science: comparisons between Northern Irish and English Schools*. Paper presented at the Annual Meeting of the British Educational Research Association, Leeds, 14–16 September.

Norwich, B. and Duncan, J. (1990). Attitudes, subjective norm, perceived preventive factors, intentions and learning science: testing a modified theory of reasoned action. *British Journal of Educational Psychology*, 60, 312–321.

National Council of Educational Research and Training (2005). *National Curriculum Framework*, NCERT, New Delhi.

Nellaippan, N.O. (1992). A Study of Scientific Attitude and Interests Among Higher Secondary Biology Students in Relation to their Learning Environment. *Fifth Survey of Educational Research,* Vol. I. 360.

Oppenheim, A.N. (1992). *Questionnaire Design Interviewing and Attitude Measurement,* Pinter Publishers, London, 197-199.

Osman, K. and Halim, L. (2002). Anchoring Science Education Towards Scientifically Literate Malayasian Society: *An Exploration of Children's Affective Psyche, University Kebangsaan, Malaysia, Bangi, Selangor, and Malaysia,* 66-69.

Oliver, J. S. and Simpson, R. D. (1988). Influences of attitude toward science, achievement motivation, and science self concept on achievement in science: a longitudinal study. *Science Education*, 72, 143–155.

Ormerod, M. (1971). The 'social implications' factor in attitudes to science. *British Journal of Educational Psychology*, 41, 335–338.

Ormerod, M. B. and Duckworth, D. (1975). *Pupils' attitudes to science* (Slough: NFER).

Osborne, J. F. and Collins, S. (2000). *Pupils' and parents' views of the school science curriculum* (London: King's College London).

Osborne, J. and Simon, S. (1996). Primary science: past and future directions. *Studies in Science Education*, 27, 99–147.

Paris, S. G. (1998). Situated motivation and informal learning. *Journal of Museum Education*, 22, 22–26.

Pell, T. and Jarvis, T. (2001). Developing attitude to science scales for use with children of ages from five to eleven years. *International Journal of Science Education*, 23, 847–862.

Potter, J. and Wetherell, M. (1987). *Discourse and social psychology: beyond attitudes and behaviour* (London: Sage Publications).

Piburn, M.D. and Baker, D.R. (1993). If I Were the Teacher. *Science Education,* 77, 393-406.

Padhi, J.S. (1994). High School Student's Science Classroom Environment and their Attitude towards Science. *School Science.* Vol. 32(3), 32-37.

Peruvian V. (1996). A Study of Attitudes of Secondary School Students towards Science. *Indian Educational Review,* Vol. 31 (2), 112-125.

Patel, V. (1998). Impact of Operational Research Technique of Network Analysis on Learning Science. *Perspective in Education,* Vol. 14. (1), 37-46.

Ponchaud, B. (2001). Primary Science: Where Next? *Paper presentation at the ASE Conference, Surrey.*

Ponte, J. P., Matos, J. F., Guimaraes, H. M., Leal, L. C. and Canavarro, A.P. (1991). Students' Views and Attitudes towards Mathematics Teaching and Leaving: *A Case Study of a Curriculum Experience,* University of Lisbon, Portugal.

Rani, S. D. (1997). A Study of Problems of Science Education and Attitude of Students towards Science in High Schools, of East Khasi Hills District, Meghalaya. *Unpublished Doctoral Dissertation, North-Eastern Hill University. Sixth Survey of Educational Research,* Vol. 1. 84.

Rao, D. B. (1990). A Comparative Study of Scientific Attitude, Scientific Aptitude and Achievement in Biology at Secondary School Level. *Fifth Survey of Educational Research,* Vol. I. 361.

Reiss, M.J. (1999). *Students, Attitudes towards Science's Long-term Perspective, Institute of Education, University of London.* 86-94.

Regan, E. and Childs, P. (2003). *An Investigation of Irish Student's Attitudes to Chemistry: The Problem in School Project.* www.google.com

Ravana, R. and Mary, A. (2008). Attitude towards Mathematics of XI Standard Students in Trichy District. *Journal of All India Association of Educational Research,* Vol. 20, Nos. 122, March-June.

Raghavan, A. (1991). Concept Mapping in Learning Physical Science and its Relation to Scholastic Performance, Cognitive Ability, Attitude Towards Concept Mapping and Science Interest Among Standard IX Students, Ph.D., Edu., University of Madras. *Fifth Survey of Educational Research,* Vol.1. 358.

Robertson, I. J. (1987). Girls and boys and practical science. *International Journal of Science Education*, 9, 505–518.

Sandman, R. S. (1973). *The development, validation, and application of a multidimensional mathematics attitude instrument.* Unpublished Doctoral thesis (Minnesota: University of Minnesota).

Schibeci, R. A. (1984). Attitudes to science: an update. *Studies in Science Education*, 11, 26–59.

Shamos, M. H. (1995). *The myth of scientific literacy* (Brunswick: NJ: Rutgers University Press).

Sharp, C., Hutchison, D., Davis, C. and Keys, W. (1996). *The take-up of advanced mathematics and science courses* (London: Schools Curriculum and Assessment Authority).

Shrigley, R. L. (1990). Attitude and behaviour are correlates. *Journal of Research in Science Teaching*, 27, 97–113.

Shulman, L. S. (1986). Those who understand: knowledge growth in teaching. *Educational Researcher*, 15, 4–14.

Simpson, R. D. and Troost, K. M. (1982). Influences of commitment to and learning of science among adolescent students. *Science Education*, 69, 19–24.

Simpson, R. D., and Oliver, J. S. (1985). Attitude toward science and achievement motivation profiles of male and female science students in grades six through ten. *Science Education*, 69, 511–526.

Simpson, R. D. and Oliver, J. S. (1990). A summary of the major influences on attitude toward and achievement in science among adolescent students. *Science Education*, 74, 1–18.

Simpson, R. D., Koballa Jr, T. R., Oliver, J. S. and Cranley, F. E. (1994). Research on the effective dimension of science learning. In D. Gabel (Ed.), *Handbook of research on science teaching and learning* (New York: Macmillan).

Sjoberg, S. (2000). Interesting all children in 'science for all'. In R. Millar, J. Leach and J. F. Osborne (Eds.), *Improving science education* (Buckingham: Open University Press), 165–186.

Smail, B. and Kelly, A. (1984). Sex differences in science and technology among 11 year old school children: II – affective. *Research in Science and Technology Education*, 2, 87–106.

Smithers, A. and Robinson, P. (1988). *The growth of mixed A-levels* (Manchester: Department of Education, University of Manchester).

Sparkes, R. A. (1995). No problem here! The supply of physics teachers in Scotland. *The Curriculum Journal*, 6, 101–113.

Sundberg, M. D., Dini, M. L. and Li, E. (1994). Decreasing course content improves student comprehension of science and attitudes toward science in freshman biology. *Journal of Research in Science Teaching*, 31, 679–693.

Stanisstreet, M. (1993). Attitudes of Children to the use of Animals. *International Journal of Science Education,* 15, 411-425

Soyibo, K. (1990). *A Comparison of Selected Lagos students' Attitudes to and Performance on a Biology Test,* 335-351.

Sandhu, R. C. (1998). School and Non- school factors, determinants. *Sixth Survey of Educational Research,* Vol. I, 84.

Sharma, P. and Shukla, P. (1999). Caste as Diagnostic Measure of Scientific Temper. *Psycho Lingua,* Vol. 29/ 9, 30-47.

Sharma, N. L. (2010). Science Attitude as a Determinant to Educational Aspiration in Students. *Unpublished Thesis in Education, Sikkim Central University.*

Sood, J. K. (1975). Attitude towards Science and Scientists. *Journal of Educational Research and Extension,* Vol. 12, No. 1, 16-19.

Sood, J. K. (1992). The Public Understanding of Science. Independent Study. Ajmer: *Fifth Survey of Educational Research,* Vol. I, 361.

Simpson, R. D. and Oliver, J. S. (1990). Attitude towards Science and Achievement Motivation Profiles of Male and Female Science Students in Grades Six through Ten. *Science Education,* 69, 511-526.

Shamai, S. (1996). Elementary School Students' Attitudes toward Science and their Course of Studies in High School from Adolescence. Provided by *Find Articles at BNET.*

Saha, S. (2007). A Study of Academic Achievement in Mathematics in Relation to Cognitive Style and Attitude towards Mathematics. Rabindra Bharati University, Kolkata.

Stephens, D. and Creaser, C. (1999). Information Science Student IT Experience and Attitude towards Computers: Results of a Five Year Longitudinal Study. Department of Information Science, Loughborough University.

Sharma, M. K. (1990). A Study of Scientific Literacy, Attitudes towards Science and Personality Traits of Students and Teachers. Ph.D., Education, University of Rajasthan, *Fifth Survey of Educational Research,* Vol.1. 361.

Srivastava, V. (1992). *A Study of Creativity among Higher Secondary Students in Relation to Scientific Aptitude and Attitude towards Science.* Ph.D., Edu. Agra University.

Suresh, T. and Rajarajeswari, N. (2005). Influence of Simulated Experiments on the Knowledge and Attitudes of Higher Secondary Students towards Bio-technology and Genetic Engineering. *Journal of All India Association for Educational Research,* Vol. 17 (3-4), Sep. – Dec., 26-29.

Sharma, I. (2008). Problem Solving Ability and Attitude towards Science as Determinant of Academic Achievement of Higher Secondary Students. *mhtnl; file :11g:\ P. / .20hd.*

Sulekha (2002). A Study of Relationship between Attitude towards Science and Learning Environment. Researches and Studies, No. 46-53, 90-91.

Tamir, P. (1990). Ethnic Origin, Sex and Science Learning of Israeli High School Students: *Studies in Educational Evaluation,* 16, 373-397.

Thabor, R. (2004). Creative Thinking Ability and Attitude towards Science among Students of Secondary School having Different Organisational Climates. Ph.D. Edu, North-Eastern Hill University, Shillong.

Temple, L. and Lips, H. (1990). Gender Differences and Similarities in Attitudes towards Computers. *Computers in Human Behaviours,* 5, 215-226.

Telli, S., Rakici, N. and Cakiroglu, J. (2000). Learning Environment and Students' Attitude towards Biology. Middle East Technical University, Faculty of Education, Department of Elementary Education, Turkey.

Talton, E. L. and Simpson, R. D. (1990). Relationships of Attitudes toward Self, Family and School with Attitude Towards science among Adolescents. *Science Education,* 70, 365-374.

Thurstone, L. L. and Chave, E. J. (1929). *The Measurement of Attitude.* Chicago University, 31-38.

Talton, E. L. and Simpson, R. D. (1985). Relationships between peer and individual attitudes toward science among adolescent students. *Science Education*, 69, 19–24.

Talton, E. L. and Simpson, R. D. (1986). Relationship of attitudes toward self, family, and school with attitude toward science among adolescents. *Science Education*, 70, 365–374.

Talton, E. L. and Simpson, R. D. (1987). Relationships of attitude toward classroom environment with attitude towards and achievement in science among tenth grade biology students. *Journal of Research in Science Teaching*, 24, 507–525.

Tarsh, J. (1994). *Young people's attitude to studying science.* Unpublished study (London: Department for Education and Employment).

Taylor, P. (1993). Minority ethnic groups and gender access in higher education. *New Community*, 19, 425–440.

Thomas, G. E. (1986). Cultivating the interest of women and minorities in high school mathematics and science. *Science Education*, 73, 243–249.

Tobias, S. (1990). *They're not dumb, they're different: stalking the second tier* (Tucson, AZ: Research Corporation).

Tobin, K. and Fraser, B. (1988). *What does it mean to be an exemplary science teacher*? Paper presented at the NARST Annual Conference, 15–17 April, San Francisco.

Turner-Bissett, R. (1999). The knowledge bases of the expert teacher. *British Educational Research Journal*, 25, 39–56.

Victor, N. H. (1935). Measuring the Scientific Attitude. *Journal of Abnormal and Social Psychology,* Vol.13,18-20.

Vidyapati, T. J. and Rao, T. V. S. (2003). Gender and Socio-Cultural Differences in Attitude towards Science, Creative Ability and Science Achievement of Ninth Grades. *Journal of Indian Education,* NCERT, New Delhi, 58-62.

Vidhate, S. N. (1997). Preparation of the Teaching Programme for Development of Scientific Attitude based on Standard VIII Science Syllabus and a Study of the Effectiveness of Programme. *Unpublished Doctoral Dissertation, Shreemati Nathibai Damodar Thackersey Women's University.*

Woodward, C. and Woodward, N. (1998). Girls and Science: does a Core Curriculum in Primary School give cause for Optimism? *Gender and Education,* 10(4).

William, J. B. (1997). Science Attitudes of Selected Middle School Students in China: A Preliminary investigation of similarities and differences as a function of gender. *An Article Published in School Science and Mathematics, Indian University,* 59-61.

Walberg, H. J. (1969). Social environment as a mediator of classroom learning. *Journal of Educational Psychology*, 60, 443–448.

Wallace, G. (1996). Engaging with learning. In J. Rudduck (Ed.), *School improvement: what can pupils tell us*? (London: David Fulton).

Watts, M. and Bentley, D. (1993). Humanising and feminising school science: reviving anthropomorphic and animistic thinking in constructivist science education. *International Journal of Science Education*, 16, 83–97.

Weinburgh, M. (1995). Gender differences in student attitudes toward science: a meta-analysis of the literature from 1970 to 1991. *Journal of Research in Science Teaching*, 32, 387–398.

Whitehead, J. M. (1996). Sex stereotypes, gender identity and subject choice at a level. *Educational Research*, 38, 147–160.

Whitfield, R. C. (1980). Educational research and science teaching. *School Science Review*, 60, 411–430.

Woodrow, D. (1996). Cultural inclinations towards studying science and mathematics. *New Community*, 22, 23–38.

Woolnough, B. (1994). *Effective science teaching* (Buckingham: Open University Press).

Yager, R. E. and Penick, J. E. (1986). Perception of four age groups toward science classes, teachers, and the value of science. *Science and Education*, 70, 355–363.

Index